# Breeder and Other Stories

# *Breeder and Other Stories*

## *Eugenia Collier*

COLLI

**DuForcelf**

# Breeder and Other Stories

*Printed on acid free paper to assure long life*

INDEXED IN

*Short Story Index 1994-1998*

Founded in 1978, Black Classic Press specializes in
bringing to light obscure and significant works by and
about people of African descent. If our books are not
available in your area, ask your local bookseller to order
them. Our current list of titles can be obtained by
writing:

Black Classic Press
c/o List
P.O. Box 13414
Baltimore, MD 21203

*A Young Press With Some Very Old Ideas*

*For my brother, H. Maceo Williams, Jr.,*
*who was also my first friend*

# Table of Contents

Marigolds .................................. 9

Ricky ...................................... 23

Breeder .................................... 67

Rachel's Children .......................... 85

A Present for Sarah ....................... 129

Journey Through Woods ................. 149

Dead Man Running ..................... 169

# *Marigolds*

**W**hen I think of the home town of my youth, all that I seem to remember is dust—the brown, crumbly dust of late summer—arid, sterile dust that gets into the eyes and makes them water, gets into the throat and between the toes of bare brown feet. I don't know why I should remember only the dust. Surely there must have been lush green lawns and paved streets under leafy shade trees somewhere in town; but memory is an abstract painting—it does not present things as they are but rather as they feel. And so, when I think of that time and that place, I remember only the dry September and the dirt roads and grassless yards of the shanty-town where I lived. And one other thing I remember, another incongruity of memory—a brilliant splash of sunny yellow against the dust—Miss Lottie's marigolds.

Whenever the memory of those marigolds flashes across my mind, a strange nostalgia comes with it and remains long after the picture has faded. I feel again the chaotic emotions of adolescence, elusive as smoke, yet as real as the potted geranium before me now. Joy and rage and wild animal gladness and shame become tangled together in the multicolored skein of 14-going-on 15, as I recall that devastating moment when I was suddenly more woman than child, years ago in Miss Lottie's yard. I think of those marigolds at the strangest times; I remember them vividly now as I desperately pass away the time waiting for you, who will not come.

I suppose that futile waiting was the sorrowful background music of our impoverished little community when I was young. The Depression that gripped the nation was no new thing to us, for the black workers of rural Maryland had always been depressed. I don't know what it was that we were waiting for; certainly not for the prosperity that was "just around the corner," for those were white folks' words, which we never believed. Nor did we wait for hard work and thrift to pay off in shining success as the American Dream promised, for we knew better than that, too. Perhaps we waited for a miracle, amorphous in concept but necessary if one were to have the grit to rise before dawn each day and labor in the white man's vineyard until after dark, or to wander about in the September dust offering one's sweat in return for a meager share of bread. But God was stingy with miracles in those days, and so we waited—and waited.

We children, of course, were only vaguely aware of the extent of our poverty. Having no radios, few newspapers and no magazines, we were somewhat unaware of the world outside our community. Nowadays we would be called "culturally deprived," and white people would write books and hold conferences about us. In those days everybody we knew was just as hungry and ill-clad as we were. Poverty was the cage in which we all were trapped, and our hatred of it was still the vague, undirected restlessness of the zoo-bred flamingo who knows instinctively that nature created it to be free.

As I think of those days I feel most poignantly the tag-end of summer, the bright dry times when we began to have a sense of shortening days and imminent cold.

By the time I was 14, my younger brother Joey and I were the only children left at our house, the older ones having left home for early marriage or the lure of the city, and the two babies having been sent to relatives who might care for them better than we. Joey was three years younger than I, and a boy, and therefore vastly inferior. Each morning our mother and father trudged wearily down the dirt road and around the bend, she to her domestic job, he to his daily unsuccessful quest for work. After our few chores around the tumble-down shanty, Joey and I were free to run wild in the sun with other children similarly situated.

For the most part, those days are ill-defined in my memory, running together and combining like a fresh watercolor painting left out in the rain. I remember squatting in the road drawing a picture in the dust, a picture which Joey gleefully erased with one sweep of his dirty foot. I remember fishing for minnows in a muddy creek and watching sadly as they eluded my cupped hands, while Joey laughed uproariously. And I remember, that year, a strange restlessness of body and of spirit, a feeling that something old and familiar was ending, and something unknown and therefore terrifying was beginning. One day returns to me with special clarity for some reason, perhaps because it was the beginning of the experience that in an inexplicable way marked the end of innocence. I was loafing under the great oak tree in our yard, deep in a reverie which I have now forgotten except that it involved secret, secret thoughts of one of the Harris boys across the yard. Joey and a bunch of kids were bored with the old tire suspended from an oak limb which had kept them entertained for awhile.

"Hey, Lizabeth," Joey yelled. He never talked when he could yell. "Hey, Lizabeth, let's go somewhere."

I came reluctantly from my private world. "Where at, Joey?"

The truth was that we were becoming tired of the formlessness of our summer days. The idleness whose prospect had seemed so beautiful during the busy school days of spring had degenerated to an almost desperate effort to fill up the empty midday hours.

"Let's go see can we find us some locusts on the hill," someone suggested.

Joey was scornful. "Ain't no more locusts there. Y'all got 'em all while they was still green."

The argument that followed was brief and not really worth the effort. Hunting locust trees wasn't fun any more.

"Tell you what," said Joey finally, his eyes sparkling "Let's us go over to Miss Lottie's."

The idea caught on at once, for annoying Miss Lottie was always fun. I was still child enough to scamper along with the group over rickety fences and through bushes that tore our already raggedy clothes, back to where Miss Lottie lived. I think now that we must have made a tragicomic spectacle, five or six kids of different ages, each of us clad in only one garment— the girls in faded dresses that were too long or too short, the boys in patchy pants, their sweaty brown chests gleaming in the hot sun. A little cloud of dust followed our thin legs and bare feet as we tramped over the barren land.

When Miss Lottie's house came into view we stopped, ostensibly to plan our strategy, but actually to reinforce our courage. Miss Lottie's house was the most ramshackle of all our ramshackle homes. The sun and rain had long since faded its rickety frame siding from white to a sullen gray. The boards themselves seemed to remain upright, not from being nailed together but rather from leaning

together like a house that a child might have
constructed from cards. A brisk wind might have
blown it down, and the fact that it was still standing
implied a kind of enchantment that was stronger
than the elements. There it stood, and as far as I
know is standing yet—a gray rotting thing with no
porch, no shutters, no steps, set on a cramped lot
with no grass, not even any weeds—a monument to
decay.

In front of the house in a squeaky rocking chair
sat Miss Lottie's son, John Burke, completing the
impression of decay. John Burke was what was
known as "queer-headed." Black and ageless, he sat
rocking day in and day out in a mindless stupor,
lulled by the monotonous squeak-squawk of the
chair. A battered hat atop his shaggy head shaded
him from the sun. Usually John Burke was totally
unaware of everything outside his quiet dream
world. But if you disturbed him, if you intruded
upon his fantasies, he would become enraged, strike
out at you, and curse at you in some strange
enchanted language which only he could
understand. We children made a game of thinking of
ways to disturb John Burke and then to elude his
violent retribution.

But our real fun and our real fear lay in Miss
Lottie herself. Miss Lottie seemed to be at least a
hundred years old. Her big frame still held traces of
the tall, powerful woman she must have been in
youth, although it was now bent and drawn. Her
smooth skin was a dark reddish brown, and her face
had Indian-like features and the stern stoicism that
one associates with Indian faces. Miss Lottie didn't
like intruders either, especially children. She never
left her yard, and nobody ever visited her. We never
knew how she managed those necessities which
depend on human interaction—how she ate, for
example, or even whether she ate. When we were
tiny children, we thought Miss Lottie was a witch,

and we made up tales, which we half believed ourselves, about her exploits. We were far too sophisticated now, of course, to believe the witch-nonsense. But old fears have a way of clinging like cobwebs, and so when we sighted the tumble-down shack, we had to stop to reinforce our nerves.

"Look, there she," I whispered, forgetting that Miss Lottie could not possibly have heard me from that distance. "She fooling with them crazy flowers."

"Yeah, look at 'er."

Miss Lottie's marigolds were perhaps the strangest part of the picture. Certainly they did not fit in with the crumbling decay of the rest of her yard. Beyond the dusty brown yard, in front of the sorry gray house, rose suddenly and shockingly a dazzling strip of bright blossoms, clumped together in enormous mounds, warm and passionate and sun-golden. The old black witch-woman worked on them all summer, every summer, while the house crumbled and John Burke rocked. For some perverse reason, we children hated those marigolds. They interfered with the perfect ugliness of the place; they were too beautiful; they said too much that we could not understand; they did not make sense. Something in the vigor with which the old woman destroyed the weeds intimidated us. It should have been a comical sight—the old woman with the man's hat on her cropped white head, leaning over the bright mounds, her big backside in the air—but it wasn't comical, it was something we could not name. We had to annoy her by whizzing a pebble into her flowers or by yelling a dirty word, then dancing away from her rage, revelling in our youth and mocking her age. Actually, I think it was the flowers we wanted to destroy, but nobody had the nerve to try it, not even Joey, who was usually fool enough to try anything.

"Y'all git some stones," commanded Joey now, and was met with instant giggling obedience as everyone except me began to gather pebbles from the dusty ground. "Come on, Lizabeth."

I just stood there peering through the bushes, torn between wanting to join the fun and feeling that it was all a bit silly.

"You scared, Lizabeth?"

I cursed and spat on the ground—my favorite gesture of phony bravado. "Y'all children git the stones. I'll show you how to use 'em."

I said before that we children were not really aware of how thick were the bars of our cage. I wonder now, though, whether we were not more aware of it than I thought. Perhaps we had some dim notion of what we were and how little chance we had of being anything else. Otherwise, why would we have been so preoccupied with destruction? Anyway, the pebbles were collected quickly, and everybody looked at me to begin the fun.

"Come on, y'all."

We crept to the edge of the bushes that bordered the narrow road in front of Miss Lottie's place. She was working placidly, kneeling over the flowers, her dark hand plunged into the golden mound. Suddenly "zing"—my expertly aimed stone cut the head off one of the blossoms.

"Who out there?" Miss Lottie's backside came down and her head came up as her sharp eyes searched the bushes. "You better git!"

We had crouched down out of sight in the bushes, where we stifled the giggles that insisted on coming. Miss Lottie gazed warily across the road for a moment, then cautiously returned to her weeding. "Zing"— Joey sent a pebble into the blooms, and another marigold was beheaded.

Miss Lottie was enraged now. She began struggling to her feet, leaning on a rickety cane and shouting, "Y'all git! Go on home!" Then the rest of the kids let loose with their pebbles, storming the flowers and laughing wildly and senselessly at Miss Lottie's impotent rage. She shook her stick at us and started shakily toward the road crying, "Black bastards, git 'long! John Burke! John Burke, come help!"

Then I lost my head entirely, mad with the power of inciting such rage, and ran out of the bushes in the storm of pebbles, straight toward Miss Lottie, chanting madly, "Old lady witch, fell in a ditch, picked up a penny and thought she was rich!" The children screamed with delight, dropped their pebbles and joined the crazy dance, swarming around Miss Lottie like bees and chanting, "Old lady witch!" while she screamed her impotent rage. The madness lasted only a moment, for John Burke, startled at last, lurched out of his chair, and we dashed for the bushes just as Miss Lottie's cane went whizzing at my head.

I did not join the merriment when the kids gathered again under the oak in our bare yard. Suddenly I was ashamed, and I did not like being ashamed. The child in me sulked and said it was all in fun, but the woman in me flinched at the thought of the malicious attack that I had led. The mood lasted all afternoon. When we ate the beans and rice that made supper that night, I did not notice my father's silence, for he was always silent these days, nor did I notice my mother's absence, for she always worked until well into evening. Joey and I had a particularly bitter argument after supper; his exuberance got on my nerves. Finally I stretched out upon the pallet in the room we shared and slipped into a fitful doze.

When I awoke, somewhere in the middle of the night, my mother had returned, and I vaguely listened to the conversation that was audible through the thin walls that separated our rooms. At first I heard no words, only voices. My mother's voice was like a cool, dark room in summer—peacefully soothing, quiet. I loved to listen to it; it made things seem all right somehow. But my father's voice cut through hers, shattering the peace.

"Twenty-two years, Maybelle, twenty-two years," he was saying, "and I ain't got nothing for you, nothing."

"It's all right, honey, you'll git something. Everybody outta work now, you know that."

"It ain't right. Ain't no man oughtta eat his woman's food day in and day out, and see his children running wild. Ain't nothing right about that."

"Honey, you took good care of us when you had it. Ain't nobody got nothing nowadays."

"I ain't talking about nobody else, I'm talking about me. God knows I try." My mother said something I could not hear, and my father cried out louder, "What must a man do, tell me that?"

"Look, we ain't starving. I git paid every week, and Miz Ellis is real nice about giving me things. She gonna let me have Mr. Ellis' old coat for you this winter—"

"God damn Mr. Ellis' coat! And God damn his money! You think I want white folks' leavings? God damn, Maybelle"—and suddenly he sobbed, loudly and painfully, and cried into the dark night. I had never heard a man cry before. I did not know that men ever cried. I covered my ears with my hands but could not cut off the sound of my father's despairing sobs. My father was a strong man who would whisk a child upon his shoulders and go singing through the house. My father whittled toys for us and laughed so loud that the great oak seemed to laugh with him, and taught us how to fish and hunt rabbits. How could it be that my father was crying? But the sobs went on unstifled, finally quieting until I could hear my mother's voice, deep and rich, humming softly as she used to hum to a frightened child.

The world had lost its boundary lines. My mother, who was small and soft, was now the strength of the family; my father, who was the rock on which the family had been built, was sobbing like the tiniest child. Everything was suddenly out of tune, like a broken accordion. Where did I fit into this crazy picture? I do not remember my thoughts, only a feeling of great bewilderment and fear.

Long after the sobbing and the humming had stopped, I lay on the pallet, still as stone, with my hands over my ears, wishing that I too could cry and be comforted. The night was silent now except for the sound of the crickets and of Joey's soft breathing. But the room was too crowded with fear to allow me to sleep, and finally, feeling the terrible aloneness of four o'clock, I decided to awaken Joey.

"Ouch! What's the matter with you? What you want?" he demanded disagreeably when I had pinched and slapped him awake.

"Come on, wake up."

"What for? Go 'way."

I was lost for a reasonable reply. I could not say, "I'm scared and I don't want to be alone," so I merely said, "I'm going out. If you want to come, come on." The promise of adventure awoke him. "Going out now? Where at, Lizabeth? What you going to do?"

I was pulling my dress over my head. Until now I had not thought of going out. "Just come on," I replied tersely.

I was out the window and halfway down the road before Joey caught up with me.

"Wait, Lizabeth, where you going?"

I was running as if the furies were after me, as perhaps they were—running silently and furiously until I came to where I had half-known I was headed: to Miss Lottie's yard.

The half-dawn light was more eerie than complete darkness, and in it the old house was like the ruin that my world had become, foul and crumbling, a grotesque caricature. It looked haunted, but I was not afraid, because I was haunted too.

"Lizabeth, you lost your mind?" panted Joey.

I had indeed lost my mind, for all of that summer's smoldering emotions swelled in me and burst—the great need for my mother who was never there, the hopelessness of our poverty and degradation, the bewilderment of being neither child nor woman and yet both at once, the fear unleashed by my father's tears. And these feelings combined in one great impulse toward destruction.

"Lizabeth!"

I leaped furiously into the mounds of marigolds and pulled madly, trampling and pulling and destroying the perfect golden blooms. The fresh smell of early morning and of dew-soaked marigolds spurred me on as I went tearing and mangling and sobbing while Joey tugged my dress or my waist crying, "Lizabeth, stop, please stop!"

And then I was sitting in the ruined little garden among the uprooted flowers, crying and crying, and it was too late to undo what I had done. Joey was sitting beside me, silent and frightened, not knowing what to say. Then, "Lizabeth, look!"

I opened my swollen eyes and saw in front of me a pair of large calloused feet; my gaze lifted to the swollen legs, the age-distorted body clad in a tight cotton night dress, and then the shadowed Indian face surrounded by stubby white hair. And there was no rage in the face now, now that the garden was destroyed and there was nothing any longer to be protected.

"M...miss Lottie!" I scrambled to my feet and just stood there and stared at her.

And that was the moment when childhood faded and womanhood began. That violent, crazy act was the last act of childhood. For as I gazed at the immobile face with the weary eyes, I gazed upon a kind of reality which is hidden to childhood. The witch was no longer a witch but only a broken old woman who had dared to create beauty in the midst of ugliness and sterility. She had been born in squalor and lived in it all her life. Now at the end of that life she had nothing except a falling-down hut, a wrecked body, and John Burke, the mindless son of her passion. Whatever verve there was left in her, whatever there was of love and beauty and joy that had not been squeezed out by life, had been there in the marigolds she had so lovingly tended.

Of course I could not express the things that I knew about Miss Lottie as I stood there awkward and ashamed. The years have put words to the things I knew in that moment, and as I look back upon it, I know that moment marked the end of innocence. Innocence involves an unseeing acceptance of things at face value, an ignorance of the area below the surface. In that humiliating moment I looked beyond myself and into the depths of another person. This was the beginning of compassion, and one cannot have both compassion and innocence.

The years have taken me worlds away from that time and that place, from the dust and squalor of our lives and from the bright thing that I destroyed in a blind childish striking out at God-knows-what. Miss

Lottie died long ago, and many years have passed since I last saw her hut, completely barren at last, for despite my wild contrition, she never planted marigolds again. Yet there are times when the image of those passionate yellow mounds returns with a painful poignancy. For one doesn't have to be ignorant and poor to find that life is barren as the dusty roads of our town. And I too have planted marigolds.

# *Ricky*

The tree stands fat and jolly, dominating the room from the usual corner. The tinsel and twinkling lights and fragile gilt balls proclaim that it is indeed Christmas. Everyone has gone now, the whole hilarious crew that drops in every year to hoist a few vessels of Christmas cheer. They were all here. All but one.

Alone and in utter silence Vi sits and feels—what? The built-in agony of family times for those of us who are alone. On the green-needled branches the twinkle-lights blink off and on in succession, making a bizarre pattern of shadows on the walls and ceiling: enormous shapes appearing and disappearing, weird distortions of familiar things. Like ghosts. Like memory. Ricky.

---

They called her fool when she took him. Fool and worse. And they were right, of course.

"Girl, you don know what you doing! How old? Eleven? Lord, you never had no child at all, and you gon keep a 'leven-year-old that been out on the street all his life? You just plain crazy!" Irma was the most outspoken, but then she would be.

Johnell was more tactful but just as firm. "You sure you thought this thing through? That little bit of money the Welfare send for these children ain't hardly worth what you gotta go through. Miz Evans down the street from me, she got six of them children, and the money don nearly pay for the wear and tear on her nerves."

Vi tried to tell them that it wasn't the money; everybody knows the Welfare doesn't make anybody rich. She told them the reasons they could understand—that she'd been alone for two years now, ever since Stick left, that she was getting on in years and needed a strong boy to work around the house, that he was, after all, almost a relative, since Aunt May had raised his father.

"Don make no difference," Irma insisted in that piercing voice of hers. "You gon have more trouble than you know what to do with."

Vi's boss, Tim Lassiter, called her fool in the roundabout way that lawyers have. His lean brown hand absently scratched at the new, not yet comfortable beard. "Not too smart an idea, Vi. Pretty risky, in fact. A kid that old, who's drifted all his life. You know how hard it is for our folks under the best of circumstances. The kid's bound to be damaged. You've typed enough of our cases to know the kinds of things that can happen."

"I knew that before I typed the first case," she snapped. She was trying to reconcile common sense with her own inner logic, and the strain was wearing on her disposition.

"I don't want to hurt your feelings, Vi, but I just don't think you're being wise."

They were right, of course, but that didn't change anything. There were reasons they didn't know about; there are things that one must do or thereafter carry the undone thing around one's neck like an albatross. One bitter cold morning years ago, a kitten froze to death on the steps of the office where she was working. She heard its painful mews when she went into the building that morning; she saw it curled miserably into a shivering gray ball in a futile struggle against the slashing wind. Vi could have taken it into the warm office with her, but she didn't. It was her first job with white people, and she wanted to make a good impression. People might laugh; her supervisor might not approve, and anyway, cats can survive the cold. But when she came out that evening, the kitten lay like a limp gray rag against the white step, no longer trembling and no longer crying, the dull eyes fixed and the red mouth gaping.

That memory must have been lying coiled in the back of her mind. It uncoiled and struck one afternoon when, by the most unlikely accident, she encountered Ricky on the courthouse elevator, wedged between an enormous, sleepy-eyed white man and the corner of the elevator. The deadpan little face seemed oddly familiar. The lusterless eyes wandered to Vi, and away, then back, and lit with a glimmer of recognition. Then she realized who he was. "Hey, aren't you Will Edwards' boy?" she asked.

The grin that broke out on his face was like a light turned on in a dark house. "Yes'm. I know you, Miss Viola."

"Ricky, what in the world are you doing here?" She glanced apprehensively at the mountainous white man who, she noticed then, had a huge forefinger hooked around Ricky's belt.

Ricky's eyes fell, and the man answered tersely, "Juvenile Court."

"Oh." The elevator stopped with a jolt, and the man was pushing his way to the front, tugging the little boy behind him. Just before the door slid shut, Ricky turned and looked at her, his eyes big in his thin dark face. It was then that she remembered, incongruously, the wail of the dying kitten.

Vi completed her errand for Mr. Lassiter and started out of the building. But Ricky's face haunted her. Her mind dredged up her few memories of Ricky. Aunt May had raised his father, Will, after Will's mother had abandoned him. Nobody ever knew anything about his father. Will was a sweet enough child, as Vi remembered. But he could never seem to get himself together and amount to anything. As the old folks say, he mean well, but he do so doggone po'. He drifted away from home when he was a teenager, didn't live anywhere. God knows how he earned a living. Every now and then he would show up at Aunt May's, hungry and dirty, stay long enough for a meal, and then drift away again. Somewhere along the line they heard that he had married, and the next time he showed up, a tiny son was toddling after him—Ricky. They saw Will and Ricky every few years, looking as much alike as two seeds from the same apple—both dirty and shabby, both thin as ghosts, both flashing the same charming smile. Vi and Aunt May used to worry about the little fellow—he was a loveable little thing who would soak up affection like a sponge—and wonder what kind of life Will was giving him. Vi wanted to take him to live with her then, but Stick wouldn't hear of it and neither would Will. She hadn't seen Ricky now for—Lord, must be three-four years. What had he been into? Where was his father? No, she couldn't just leave him in Juvenile Court. She turned and went back.

Getting into Juvenile Court wouldn't be any problem. After all, she was almost a relative, and besides, Tim Lassiter's name could get you into almost anyplace in Baltimore. She went into the waiting room and sat down quietly in the back.

She scanned the room for Ricky. The room was a patchwork quilt of troubled people: kids tense and shaken, grown people worried and guilt-ridden, social workers and lawyers sleek, well-dressed and eager get their cases over with. Ricky sat near the front, next to the red-faced man who escorted him.

From where she sat Ricky was a shrunken little figure—head down, shoulders drooping forward, still as death.

It was close to an hour before Ricky's case was called. Meanwhile, she sat there and remembered the sessions she had attended in Juvenile Court with Mr. Lassiter's clients. The hearings are held privately in a room which tries to look friendly and intimate but really looks as menacing as the grin of an enemy. The children she'd seen there had been truly the city's stepchildren. The city's benevolent agents—probation workers, social workers, and a clean white judge—descended upon them like buzzards upon carrion. Not that the judge was unkind. Not that anybody was unkind. It's just that they all seemed unrelated to the real trauma of the young lives whose direction was now in their hands. The social workers' reports followed a format, used the same jargon, reduced each case to a kind of formula. The judge, with enviable precision, crisply disposed of each case, and the child was led away, wide-eyed and silent or tearful and hysterical, and the case was over. The whole thing was rather like a hideous game in which the stakes are children's lives. Or so it seemed to her now.

When they called Ricky, she felt a wave of heat flow over her. She gripped her purse. She caught a glimpse of Ricky's face as he and the white guard lumbered toward the hearing room. His thin little face was expressionless, like a bottle from which all the wine has been poured. His shoulders still sagged, and his arms dangled lifelessly as he walked.

Vi hesitated a second and then followed them to the thick door of the hearing room. She was admitted after she explained to the bailiff that she was distantly related to the child. She took her seat with the others in front of the shiny desk behind which sat the judge. Sat God. Old as hell, his hair and face the same dead white, his eyes covered by round eyeglasses that reflected the light and concealed his eyes. Dispensing Justice in a high, querulous voice.

"Lord have mercy!" She said to herself. "It's Judge Harmon!" Vi remembered with distaste Judge Harmon's superior attitude the last time she had had business in his court—she was taking notes for Mr. Lassiter in a domestic relations case. The old man wore his black robes as if they conferred in him a kind of holiness that put him far above the erring folk who came before him. Vi remembered his open contempt for the people he faced, especially the black people, his failure to grasp the plight of the women whose estranged men were not supporting them, and most of all, his subtle jeering at one particular couple who had apparently come before him on other occasions. In this last instance, he had played the straight man to the hilt, asking just the right questions to elicit answers that would lead to giggles from the rows of ghouls who spent their days being entertained by other people's troubles. And the couple played right along with him like Rastus and Mandy in a coon show. But the judgment went in their favor. Judge Harmon was not wearing his black robes today in juvenile court, but he still wore the air of Almighty God.

Ricky's eyes widened with surprise when he saw Vi; the familiar grin flickered for a second on the corners of his mouth, then disappeared as his features settled back into the opaque mask.

Vi listened attentively to the report of the probation officer, a well-dressed young beige-colored man whose clean fingers held the papers as if they were holding something dirty. He read in a smooth crisp ivy league voice. Beneath the jargon, Vi surmised that the actual hearing had been held some weeks ago and an investigation subsequently made. Ricky had been returned to court from the training school for disposition of the case.

In that proper, well-oiled voice, Ricky's whole sordid history was laid out before the court. Ricky's early years had been spent with his father, living in the streets, sleeping in unlocked cars or empty houses, eating whenever and whatever they could, wearing whatever clothes came their way. *O Lord, didn't I remember?* At six Ricky was past expert at panhandling and pilfering. When he was eight his father disappeared. Ricky was found one December morning crouched in the vestibule of a responsible Negro citizen, who called the radio car, which carted him off to Pine Street Station, where he became the child of the city Welfare Department. In the ensuing three years he had lived in eight foster homes but had adjusted to none. He became a truant and a chronic runaway. After the last episode the Welfare Department had referred him to Juvenile Court as a delinquent minor. He had been sent to Boys' Village until some disposition could be made. Meanwhile, no trace of his father had been uncovered either in public records or in the flesh. His mother had been found, however—a long-term patient in a state mental hospital, with no memory whatsoever of a little boy named Ricky.

Vi was deeply moved by the businesslike recitation of the little fellow's life. Her mind filled in the blanks—the fear, the rage, the loneliness, the strength it had taken for mere survival. Her teeth were clenched so tight that her jaw was beginning to ache. *Why didn't me and Aunt May know? Why didn't anybody tell us?*

The judge asked Ricky to come to the desk. It was an odd confrontation—the thin little black boy and the pale old man with centuries of righteousness endowed by the invisible robes.

"Well, Richard," Judge Harmon began, his eyeglasses beaming like headlights under the glaring lights of the courtroom. "I must decide what to do with you. It's not an easy decision."

The judge paused as if he expected an answer, so Ricky, his head high, murmured, "Yes sir."

"Tell me, Richard, why do you keep running away?"

Ricky was silent. Vi couldn't see his face, but she imagined that his expression was still totally blank. His hands down at his sides were clenched into fists.

"Well, Richard?"

"I don't know, sir." *The law of the jungle—don't let the enemy know what's going on inside of you. And like Aunt May used to tell me, always talk respectful to white folks—they don't know how to fight respect.*

The judge probably knew from past experience with street-hardened boys that he wasn't going to get any more out of him. Besides, he had given him his chance.

"Well," Judge Harmon said finally, "we have given you everything that our foster care has to offer—and you have used none of it. I really don't see what we can offer you now except Boys Village until you come of age or until some other plan can be made. Does anyone have anything else to say?" It was almost a rhetorical question. The probation officer began gathering up his papers. The judge's eyeglasses threw back the stark white light of the courtroom.

In a split second Vi told herself all the things that Johnell and Irma would tell her later. No, she concluded, there was nothing she could do.

"Your Honor," she heard herself saying as she rose from her chair, "I would be willing to take this child."

The judge turned to her with a jerk. The probation officer froze. Ricky's face was undecipherable.

"Please come forward," Judge Harmon managed to say.

*Look what you got yourself into now! I thought to myself, you gon have more trouble than Dick's dog got fleas!*

Vi heard herself give her name and occupation, her past knowledge of the child, and her reasons for believing (hoping) she could cope with him. The probation officer agreed that there was a possibility that even without a husband she could be acceptable as Ricky's foster mother. And after all, what else would they do with him?

There was a bit of parrying back and forth among them as Judge Harmon asked the probation worker and Vi the expected questions and got, apparently, the appropriate answers. Finally the judge turned and looked squarely at Ricky and Vi standing side by side in front of him. Vi could see his eyes now—severe and blue and cold.

"All right, then, you can take him pending investigation by the Welfare Department."

"Now?" she gasped. Things were moving so fast she couldn't keep up with them.

"Certainly. Or is there something you're not telling us?"

Vi glanced at Ricky. She didn't want to jeopardize anything. But *Lord have mercy, how did they expect me to take on a child just like that, with no preparation? The spare room was a mess. And anyway, Judge Harmon didn't know the first thing about me, not really. How could he just give a child away like that?* But when she peered again into those cold blue eyes, the answer was obvious.

As they left the court house a few minutes later, dazed and silent, Vi didn't know who was more amazed, Ricky or herself. Or Mr. Lassiter, when she returned to work nearly two hours late, towing a brand new son.

Ricky didn't really come alive until they got home. "Come on, man, ain't nothing to be scared of," Vi said heartily, slipping out of her "educated" English and into the smooth lingo with which black people speak to each other when they are alone, as easily and naturally as a woman coming home from work slips out of a stiff girdle and into a warm, comfortable robe.

Ricky had been to Vi's house before, of course, had even spent a night or two there. But this was different. For awhile he stood around awkwardly, not knowing what to do. But he soon responded to her warmth. While Vi fixed dinner he perched on the stool in the kitchen and listened to the music on her portable radio and chattered to Vi during the commercials.

After dinner they came to grips with the fact of their living together. Vi ran down the jobs he would have to do around the house—"I been doing these things since Stick left—it's good to have a man to do them now"—and he flashed that grin of his. And they talked about his privileges: "Soon as the Welfare tells us something about the money, we'll see about an allowance for you. I'm—things are kinda tight right now." And they sketched out his daily routine. Vi called Aunt May to see whether Ricky could stay with her while Vi was at work. When Vi told her that Ricky was with her now, there was a long silence on her end of the phone. Vi could imagine the look on Aunt May's face—mouth open, eyes wide and unbelieving. After a moment she said, "Do Jesus!" But she promised to help.

Hours later when the house was finally silent, Vi lay thinking how good it would be to live with someone again—to not be alone. She fell asleep with all sorts of plans spinning in her head, not aware of the problems gathering like dark clouds that would shortly rain heartache upon them. Having no clairvoyance to show her the nights of agonized tossing and turning. The first night, Vi slept.

---

The most immediate problem became acute the next morning: clothes. Ricky had come to her with nothing but the clothes on his back. Where were his things?

It took Vi four days to track down the Welfare worker, who was seldom at his desk and didn't believe in returning calls. He said that Ricky's possessions were probably at the last foster mother's house.

"Can you get them for me?"

"Well, no, actually I can't." It seems that the case had only recently been transferred to him from Long-term Care; he was in Institutional Care. Now that Ricky would not be in an institution, the case was in transit back to Long-term Care. Vi should call back one day next week when the transfer was completed, and Central Files would give her the name of the new worker. *I was really sick of him—all this who-struck-John about Long-term Care and Institutional Care and all that shit, and here was this child naked as a picked sparrow in whistletime!*

"What does he wear in the meantime?"

"Mrs. Coleman, I really can't help you," replied the clipped New England voice. "It's not my case."

*I'd've got them my damn self if Ricky had been able to remember the address.*

When she called back the following week, she was told that Ricky's case had been transferred to an uncovered caseload—she would be notified when someone was hired to cover it.

Fortunately, Vi hadn't waited for the Welfare Department to act. Along with their predictions of disaster, Irma and Johnell brought out their boys' outgrown shirts and pants and underwear. Ricky was delighted.

"Aunt Vi, look at me!" He flew into the kitchen where Irma and Vi were having a beer. He was wearing a red shirt donated by Irma's Roy. He strutted around like a young rooster, his eyes shining, the brilliant red of the shirt bringing a rich glow to his dark skin. *Sharp as Dick when Hattie died!*

Irma was tickled. "Honey," she chuckled, "I'm sure glad he's young enough to be my grandchild. He gon be something with the women, and I always did like them good-looking men!"

In general Ricky and Vi were making it pretty well together. The simplest things pleased him, things that most children take for granted. An Apache scarf from the 5 & 10, a dish of ice cream at night, an old pair of sunglasses—almost any little thing evoked that special grin. And Vi began to see herself in a different perspective. *I don't have much in the way of material things, and I've scratched for what I do have but Lord I've forgotten what it's like to be really poor.*

He never talked much about his past, but every now and then some hint of it would surface, and Vi realized again the extent of his desolation. Like the day she brought home the apples. She'd seen them in the market red, firm, juicy—she brought home a bagful. When she set them out on the table in a bowl, Ricky just looked at them wistfully.

"Aunt Vi," he whispered, "Can I have one?"

She was busy getting dinner. "Sure, I got them for you, man!"

His eyes were gazing into some other time and some other place. He took an apple and sat there looking at it.

"Hey, they for eating, not looking," she said cheerily. But his face was such a study—"What's wrong, Rick?"

He came back to the present, his small face still serious. "I 'member the last time I had a apple like this, a old lady gimme it for carrying her shopping bag. It sure looked good."

He paused. She stopped stirring the gravy. "What's the matter, didn't it taste good? Did it have worms?"

He shrugged. "I taken it home, and my foster mother she taken it and say I shouldn't 'cept nothing from strangers. But later on, I seen her give my apple to her son."

He recited it almost like a lesson. *If I could've gotten hold of that foster mother, I'd've snatched a knot in her ass.* Ricky finally took a big bite out of the apple, but Vi knew that all the red apples in Lexington Market couldn't give back the one thing that had been his and that a heedless adult had taken away.

More than once—repeatedly, in fact—Vi felt an overwhelming sadness and frustration as she sensed the extent of his loss—not apples, no, but some vital portion of humanness. From below the sunny exterior of his delight with little things, the problems surfaced one by one, like ugly and dangerous sea creatures breaking the surface of a glassy bay.

They faced the first problem from the very first morning: Ricky was a bed-wetter.

During the mad rush out of the house in time to take him to Aunt May's before she went to work, she glanced hurriedly into his room and noticed that the bed was shoddily made. "Have to show him how," Vi muttered to herself, snatching the covers back. And then she saw it—a large damp circle, drying yellow at the edge. *Oh my God, poor little thing, he was trying to hide it!* She ached with compassion. She had no idea how to handle this problem. She knew only one thing: the sheets had to be washed. She jerked them off the bed, threw them down the basement steps and rushed out to work.

The sheets were in the washing machine when Ricky rang the doorbell that evening, aglow from a merry day with Aunt May. "Hi, Aunt Vi, me and Aunt May had hot dogs and potato chips for lunch today!"

Vi let him tell her about his day, then she cautiously approached the subject they had to discuss.

"Rick, I put some clean sheets out for you. If the mattress is dry, you can make up your bed before dinner."

His face died. "Oh. Yes'm."

He turned to go upstairs, but she knew they had to talk this thing out. She put her hand on his arm. He flinched; he hated to be touched. "It's okay, Rick. Look, how often do you—does this happen?"

He was looking down at the floor. "Most every night."

Vi explained that children sometimes did that when they were nervous and that when he'd gotten used to being here, that wouldn't happen any more.

"What did your last foster mother do when it happened?"

"Sometimes she just hollered." Softly, "Sometimes she hit me."

"Well, I won't do that. We'll work it out. Just put the sheets in the washing machine for me whenever it happens. You know where the clean sheets stay." He started up the stairs. She wanted him to feel unashamed. "Everything's cool, man!" Vi called after him.

They talked about it frankly after that. And they tried everything. No liquids after six o'clock, no fruit, she even thought of getting one of those devices she had seen advertised. Finally, they hit on a routine that worked some of the time, at least: Vi got him up every two hours to go to the bathroom. It was wearing on them both, but their reward was the occasional mornings when Ricky would bounce out of bed squawking triumphantly, "Aunt Vi! Aunt Vi! I didn't wet last night!"

They never did get the problem solved entirely. Even when his days were good, at night the fears of all his life came stealing out from the dark recesses of his mind and reminded him—reminded her— that for this child there would be no peace.

Ricky had been living with her for nearly three weeks when Vi received a call from the Welfare Department in the form of one Miss Holtz. She thought at first that Miss Holtz was the long-awaited worker who would track down Ricky's clothes for them, but Miss Holtz explained that no, someone from Long-term Care would have to do that; she was the Intake worker who would have to come out and approve Vi's home.

From her thin, reedy voice, Vi pictured Miss Holtz as a thin, reedy person. Instead, she turned out to be a boxy woman with short stringy blond hair and an authoritative manner. Vi could see that she had been in the welfare business for a long time.

She inspected the whole house, her colorless eyes probing each room for something amiss, her nervous fingers making quick notes on a little pad. Vi liked her less with each room. She was particularly interested in Ricky's room.

"This isn't very large for a growing boy," she informed Vi severely.

Vi thought about her own childhood in Virginia, where the lucky children slept three in a bed and the others slept on the floor. "Ricky seems to like it," she snapped. "At least it's all his own."

Vi looked around the room, satisfied herself. Surprisingly, Ricky kept the room very neat—perhaps because he had so few possessions to clutter it. Under the plain cotton spread were fresh sheets—last night's sheets were hanging on the line in the basement.

Miss Holtz's thin voice was now covered with a coating of honey. "Oh, I'm sure he does, Mrs. Coleman. It's just that every child needs a certain amount of space in which to grow. Our manual clearly specifies this. Can you tell me the dimensions of the room?"

Vi told her.

"Oh, no, that's not enough. Well, we'll see, maybe we can make do." Her thin lips arranged themselves into a smile of sorts.

After the inspection, they sat in the living room and talked. She wanted to know all about Vi's background. Vi thought of the years in Virginia, of Big Ma, whose love was a warm cocoon until she died of poverty and neglect in Vi's thirteenth year, of Aunt May who brought Vi to live with her in Baltimore after nobody at home had room for "Walter's side child." But she wasn't going to tell Miss Holtz all these things. She answered the loaded questions truthfully but as scantily as possible. In spite of Miss Hotlz's apparent skill and diplomacy, Vi felt that she was feeding information into a computer.

Miss Holtz wanted to know all about Vi's present employment and about her marital status. How does one explain the breakup of a twenty-year marriage? Vi didn't try. But in wispy seconds she relived the struggle, the toil, the trap that was the city, the tawdry ways Stick had of proving his manhood, the final fight, the final break...Stick....

"What are your present relations with Mr. Coleman?" Vi tried to explain that Stick was totally irrelevant to her plans regarding Ricky. Miss Holtz seemed skeptical, but she wrote it all down.

She wanted to know about Vi's relations with men. Vi thought she was searching for a father figure for Ricky; she told her that really, she didn't have or want a steady boyfriend. Even with the next series of questions, Vi didn't get her drift.

"Mrs. Coleman, I do appreciate your frankness. Now I want you to tell me just as frankly, why did you volunteer to take Ricky?"

That was a tough one to feed into a computer. "As I said, I knew him and his father before—they're really like relatives. And besides, I thought I could help him. And I'm alone here—he'll be company."

Her eyes lit up. "Let's pursue that idea. You want him to provide company for you because you're lonely?"

Vi wasn't aware of her subtle shift from *alone* to *lonely*. "Well—partly."

"Yes," Miss Holtz said sympathetically, "after being married for all those years and now not having a husband or a boyfriend, I can see that you'd be *lonely*."

Again—that subtle shift from "no steady boyfriend" to "without a boyfriend."

"Tell me," she continued smoothly, "is that why you wanted a male child? To fulfill the role of the man of the house?"

Vi got it now. Her emphasis on man gave her away. *I have some raunchy friends, but this clean blond woman sitting in my living room seemed so foul, so dirty that I wanted to throw her out on her ass.*

But Vi played it cool, because she had something at stake. "Miss Holtz, I have no plans for screwing an eleven-year-old. Now write *that* down on your pad."

Miss Holtz was as cool as Vi was, except for the decided flush to the roots of her blond hair. "I didn't say that, Mrs. Coleman. You did."

The interview was over. She left, clinging to her note pad. *White folks—Lord, you got to watch them every minute. Bitch!* Vi slammed the door and stood there fuming.

Miss Holtz had neither seen Ricky nor asked to see him.

Vi's next contact with the Welfare Department was, at least, pleasant. The new worker was a nice little thing named Miss Clewell, fresh from college, all of twenty-two years old. She was tiny, hardly taller than Ricky. Her hair fell in soft dark ringlets around a rosy little face with soft hazel eyes. *She looked like a young person who had folks, you know—like somebody who had been taken care of for all her life.* Later, Vi remembered thinking, that first day when she and Ricky and Miss Clewell sat in the living room talking, that there was no way for this clean white child to have any idea what their world, Ricky's and Vi's, was really like. No way. But at least she was pleasant.

The summer passed quickly, and Ricky blossomed like a flower in the sun. He put on weight, and the dark circles under his eyes began to fade. His skin became clear and healthy. He was wearing his hair in an Afro now—the last foster mother made him keep it short because she didn't want her children to look like "them bad niggers out in the street."

It was a beautiful summer for Vi. He made her see things through different eyes—the joy that lies hidden in the most ordinary things. Johnell and Irma both had kids his age, and it took only a phone call for them all to be off on some outing or other. And whatever they did was new to Ricky. *My Lord, I kept thinking, how can I fill this many empty spaces?* On his first trip to the beach he just lay at the water's edge, laughing, and let the waves lap over him. On his first train ride he stared fascinated as the scenery whipped past. On his first trip to an amusement park he wanted to ride on everything, even the kiddie rides. He was hungry for life, like someone snatched from the grave.

But at night the fear returned, and almost invariably, in spite of their precautions, the morning revealed the same circle of wet.

As school time approached, another problem surfaced.

One evening in late August, Vi was fixing a hurried dinner after a day of sightseeing in Annapolis. It had been one of those emotionally draining days, and her mind hovered over its details as her hands peeled potatoes and shaped hamburgers. Ricky had been enthralled with the Naval Academy. They had traveled the green campus burgeoning with summer flowers, peered into the enormous dormitory, gazed reverently at the crypt containing John Paul Jones' long dead bones, giggled at the war paint on the marble Tecumseh, marveled at the relics in the museum, looked longingly at the sailboats scudding across the bay. The midshipmen striding along in their summer uniforms had seemed to Ricky the greatest people in the world. Vi's own heart had reached out warmly to a jaunty black mid whose smooth skin was like brown satin against the gleaming white tropical shirt. As they passed each other he had grinned at Ricky and winked. Ricky cried, "Aunt Vi, when I git big I'm going to this school!" *That poor little face looking at me, those eyes just shining like that—wanting so hard—*

Fixing dinner, Vi thought of the doors to his future that were already closed to him, how far out of his reach was the American Dream. Better get her mind on the potatoes she was frying; they, at least, were tangible and real and immediate.

"Rick, go get me a can of apple sauce out of the cupboard." He'd like that for dessert.

"Okay," he called from the living room, where he was watching cartoons on TV. In a minute he handed her a can and started back to his program.

"No, baby, the apple sauce. Take this back and bring the apple sauce." He had brought a can of crushed corn. "Oh, and while you're there, bring me that little bag of flour," she called after him.

This time he brought the apple sauce, but instead of flour, he brought corn meal. Vi kidded him a little. "Hey, man, you didn't wash your ears this morning. You know good and well that *flour* don't sound nothing like *corn meal*."

He was flustered and unhappy. "Ain't that flour?" he demanded.

"No, baby, look, there it is on the bag. What's that say?"

He glanced at the words which for him were meaningless. "I guess it say flour."

*I knew then that he couldn't read a lick. Eleven years old—Sweet Jesus—and got to look at the picture on the label to see what's in the can!*

Little Miss Clewell couldn't help. She was astonished. "Honestly, Mrs. Coleman, there's not a thing in his record to indicate that he can't read. She looked like a little doll sitting there on that faded old over-stuffed chair—a wax doll in a perky pink dress.

Across from her, Vi flicked the ash off her cigarette and took another long drag, inhaling deeply. "Just what does the record say about school?"

"Nothing about any learning problems—just about his behavior problems. There've been quite a few." Her hazel eyes were grave.

"Yes, I understand that, Miss Clewell, but didn't the other foster mothers say anything about his trouble reading? Weren't there any conferences with the teachers? I mean, there's got to be something."

"But there isn't."

"Well, how did he manage to pass?"

"He's been in these ungraded schools where you don't pass from one grade to another."

"Well, if this isn't one mess!"

When she went back to the office, Miss Clewell searched the record for any testing that had been done. She reported to Vi that different IQ tests showed him to be mildly retarded, severely retarded, and low normal. "So take your choice," she muttered angrily.

Vi could only repeat, "Well, if this isn't one mess!"

Ricky was to attend an ungraded school not too far away. He had attended that school two years back and was acquainted with the principal, whose office he had occupied frequently, and with some of the teachers. He knew the teacher to whom he had been assigned.

"She nice," he assured Vi, "not like that old Miss Grinnage that I had before. She make you do your work, though."

So Vi felt some reassurance as school time approached.

There would be some adjustments, however. They talked about it one night in the kitchen after dinner, as Vi sipped her coffee and Ricky sat with his long legs akimbo and his arms flung on the back of the chair.

"You won't have to go to Aunt May's any more when school starts."

"Oh, can't I go after school?" Ricky and Aunt May's dog Big Boy had become fast friends.

"Well, sometimes. But we got to save carfare. Best you come on home most days. I won't be long getting home after you do."

"Aunt Vi, how I'm gon git in?"

Vi had thought for a long time about whether to give Ricky a key. His life had been so haphazard up to now and a lost key is a serious matter—but you have to start trusting a child somewhere along the line. "Tell you what, man. I think it's time for you to have a key of your own."

"Wow, no stuff!" He had never had a key, not to any door.

They talked for awhile about the responsibility of having a key. "This is our home," she said seriously, "and we got to protect it, so never lose this key or misuse it, see?" She concluded warmly, "I want you to have a key to this door—always."

*He sat there in the kitchen—it smelled good in there—looking first at the key and then at me. Just grinning that grin of his. You'd a thought I'd given him a bundle of money. I wanted so bad to go hug him close, but I knew how he hated for anybody to touch him. So I just sat there, on the other side of the table, grinning just like him.*

After a few minutes Vi felt close enough to ask him something that had been bothering her. "Rick, tell me something. Why'd you run away from those other homes?"

His grin faded, and his face became serious. Vi had a feeling that he was struggling to express something for which he had no vocabulary. "Well, I guess—uh—" then silence.

"You don't have to tell me if you don't want to."

"Aunt Vi, I just didn't like them people."

"Not any of them?"

"Not much." Silence again. Vi finished her coffee, and he sat staring thoughtfully at the key. "And anyway, Aunt Vi, I had to look for my father."

"You were looking for Will Edwards? Well, Lord a'mighty!" He looked up at Vi, his eyes glittering fiercely. "Oh, Ricky," she went on softly, "How could you expect to find him when the police couldn't?"

"They didn't know where to look."

For a moment they just sat there. There was no sound except the hum of the refrigerator and the bark of a distant dog. At last Vi leaned over. "He'll come back one day, honey, yes he will. He'll look up Aunt May like he always does, and she'll tell him where you are. Rick, he'll come back." *And if he does I'll put my foot in his ass, the no good black bastard.* "This is your home now, Rick. We making it together, man."

She reached over and touched his hand. He jumped, as if her touch had burned. He pushed back his chair, his face once more a lifeless mask. "I got to go upstairs."

By the next day he was cheerful again. In spite of everything, Vi was optimistic about the coming school year. Ricky already liked the teacher, and somehow they would work together to overcome the reading problem. Vi was chronically tired from getting him up every two hours at night, but somehow she would find the energy to help. But the night before the opening of school something happened that cast a shadow over their joyful plans.

Ricky had been particularly buoyant when he got home from Aunt May's and had chattered away about school all through dinner. When the phone rang, he was upstairs looking over his meager wardrobe (Miss Clewell had finally located his clothes) to find something special for school.

"Vi—Vi—Oh, Lord—" It was Aunt May, crying.

"Aunt May, what's happened?" All the dreadful possibilities flashed through Vi's mind.

"Vi, Big Boy laying in the alley dead."

She was crying so hard Vi had to make her repeat it. "Oh my Lord, Aunt May, what happened to him?"

"He just laying there with his mouth open and his tongue out on the ground with the end of it bit near off." Vi could hardly make out what she was saying. "And his eyes popping out."

"Oh, what happened?"

"I don't know, I don't know. Musta been them bad boys opened the back gate again and let him out and done something to him. I don't know."

"When did it happen? Did anybody see?"

"Nobody seen nothing, at least nobody I axed. Musta been right after Ricky left 'cause him and Ricky was playing in the yard last time I seen him. He was such a nice little dog, Vi. Never hurt nobody. Poor Ricky, he gon be all tore up." Vi felt cold all over. So much violence, so many losses in one short life—poor little Ricky—how would this affect him? Vi comforted Aunt May as best she could, enraged that the friendly, trusting little dog should be so cruelly violated.

Just as she hung up the phone, Ricky came clattering down the stairs. Quietly she told him what had happened. *His face—what kind of face was that? His hands grabbing that chair so tight the knuckles near 'bout coming through the skin. But his face didn't say nothing.* "I feel so bad, Ricky. He was—well—gentle. Why would anybody do that to him?" Ricky gripped the sides of his chair.

Neither of them said anything for awhile, but the room seemed somehow crowded with noise. Finally, Ricky took a deep breath and let go the chair. His face was a weird grimace. He shrugged, got ready to speak but changed his mind, turned and crept upstairs to his room. Vi went up a little later, but the door was closed.

That night Vi got him up as usual. But the next morning the sheets were soaking

*It was a bad sign, Big Boy's death. I knew it— something inside warned me, just as clear as a voice telling me to beware. But I wouldn't listen, couldn't hear. Because by that time I loved the child.*

---

Things seemed to go well for awhile. From being a loner, Ricky suddenly blossomed forth into a social butterfly. He had a natural charisma which drew other children to him, and soon the afternoons and Saturdays were filled with little boys.

There seemed to be hope for the reading problem. Ricky's teacher, Mrs. Connor, was a big dark-skinned woman who operated at just the right place between the poles of strictness and permissiveness. She was vitally interested in Ricky and eager to give Vi the kind of guidance she needed to help him at home. She lent him materials that were interesting but simple enough to be within his reach.

"It would be insulting to give him Dick and Jane," she explained.

Vi and Ricky worked on the reading every night, and slowly, painfully, they made progress. Each new word was a victory; each sentence comprehended was a triumph. Along with the reading, they practiced writing. Ricky had surprisingly good handwriting for his stage of development. He soon began to copy things from his reading materials and finally branched out to writing words and even composing short sentences. One day Vi found a finger-marked little slip of paper on which was written seven times in round, labored letters, "I love Will Edwards."

Autumn seemed particularly beautiful that year. On Sundays after church, Vi and Ricky would take long bus rides into the country and then get out and walk a little in the gentle autumn sun. There had been so little of nature in Ricky's life; he delighted in every brilliant tree, every flower, every bee gathering the last of the nectar before the cold that would surely come. One afternoon in late October, as they stood admiring a bright splash of marigolds against an evergreen bush, Vi thought of how nature lets some things bloom at the end of the year, and she thought of her life which was blossoming now in its own autumn, but she had no words to say this to Ricky. He seemed to sense her feelings, for he murmured, "Oh, Aunt Vi, ain't they pretty?" Vi gave him a quick hug, and this time he didn't flinch.

He began to be involved in frequent fights, some of them extremely vicious and most of them involving boys with whom he had been friendly. The reasons for the fights were never quite clear—" He say my father a punk"—"he say he gon beat my ass"—"He threw my books in the gutter." It was as if he could let human affection get only so close to him, and then he must push it away, destroy it. Charisma and cruelty intermingled in him so that those who were charmed today were attacked tomorrow. There was, for him, no love without hate.

Vi was beginning to notice all sorts of confusing contradictions in him. He still could not bear to be touched—except for that one moment on an autumn hill—but kept the door to his room open, as if he also couldn't bear to be alone. He plugged away patiently at his reading and writing but flew into a rage if he couldn't find his football. And the days when he went to school sunny and smiling were the days when his behavior at school was the most intolerable.

The conferences with the principal and teacher were unending. Knowing his background, they were sympathetic, but they were also firm.

"Mrs. Coleman, I have a roomful of problem children," Mrs. Connor remarked once. "I like children with problems—I used to be one myself. I can say that now. So my children are really special to me. But Ricky is the fuse that sets them all off."

The principal, a thin, aging man, put in, "Yes, the truth is probably that he's a born leader. But he's so damaged himself that he leads them into trouble—he can really influence those children."

"Manipulate them, you mean," said Mrs. Connor.

They decided that they would have to use the right combination of patience and punishment (and love! and love!), and time would straighten him out.

There were isolated days when things seemed to be working, and seeing Ricky's laughing face, Vi could not believe in the ghost that lay behind his eyes. Thanksgiving, the cousins gathered at Aunt May's, and for an evening Ricky was part of a family. *And when Uncle Lonnie asked the blessing I didn't bow my head—I couldn't. I looked at each one of them, the old ones, sick and work-worn and never had nothing, the young ones scratching for a way, and then I looked at Ricky, and I wished to hell them damn Pilgrims had stayed home and let us stay in Africa. Christmas. He looked so good in that gold sports jacket. Never even had a Christmas tree before. Hung up his stocking like a little kid. And for once Christmas was good, not the awful thing people have*

*made it. That week we got snowed in. Sliding down
the hill on some kid's sled, waving at me and yelling.*

And Alfy. One bitter cold day in February, Vi
didn't get a chance to call out, "Rick, I'm home." He
was waiting in the hall by the door. "Aunt Vi, come
here, I got something to show you!"

He was so excited she didn't even take off her
coat but followed him into the basement.

"Look, Aunt Vi, look!"

It was the saddest looking dog Vi had ever seen.
It lay on a pile of rags by the furnace, still shivering
as if the cold had accumulated inside its frail body.
Its ribs stuck out like an accordion. Its sparse hair
was no color at all. Its tail and head drooped.

"Well, do Jesus, Ricky, what is this?"

"He was standing on the corner when I got off
the bus. He cold, and he ain't got no place to sleep
tonight." Ricky's eyes were big and bright. Was he
thinking of those nights he and his father had slept
in cars and empty houses? "Can't we let him stay
here? I can take care of him."

Vi did some quick mental arithmetic with cost of
dog food, the possibility of fleas, and assorted
matters. They added up to no. But then Ricky had
missed Big Boy so, and maybe if he had something to
love....

So Alfy became a member of the household.
Ricky did take care of him with real devotion. In
time, Alfy's hair grew into a luxuriant red-brown, his
eyes began to glow; his tail became a cheerful
waving fluff. He and Ricky became a steady team,
and no matter what trouble Ricky had in school,
with Alfy he was always gentle.

Early in March, Ricky was suspended from
school. He had beaten a child with the buckle end of
a belt. Fortunately, two male teachers had
interceded before the child was severely hurt. The

child had called Ricky a girl-boy and had pushed him. Vi hurried over to the school, where the principal told her what had happened.

By the time she got home, she was furious. She had tried so hard, been so patient, and now she just didn't know what to do. He was coming up out of the basement when she slammed the door behind her. His smile was sunny and innocent.

"You little bastard, what the hell you think you doing, beating somebody with a goddamn belt!" Her fury burst like a summer storm. Her words were like shotgun pellets as she ranted on and on. His face abandoned the smile and became a mask again. And the cardboard countenance accelerated her fury until without warning to him or even to herself, she slapped him hard across the face.

With the sharp crack of her hand in his flesh, the mask dropped, and she recoiled at the blazing hatred. He struck out at her once, aiming for her breast, but she turned and hard knuckles jabbed into her arm. She cried out, lost her balance, and fell hard against the wall. He roared like a blood hot animal and dashed from the house.

She did not see him again for nearly two weeks. Even months later her mind could only gloss over the anguish of those days, picking up sad little splinters of memory. The self-blame. The dead silence of the house. The endless days. The impossible nights. And the attitudes of other people.

Miss Clewell: "Why, sure you're concerned, you've got to be concerned. But the police will find him, you can be sure of that. And he can survive, Mrs. Coleman. He's street-wise."

Johnell: "Try not to worry, honey. Maybe it's just as well." Irma: "I told you so—didn't I tell you.—I told you, sure as shooting—"

And the frightful images in her own mind.

Then one Sunday he came back. Dirty, tousled, but jaunty and smiling. Vi was sitting in the kitchen staring blankly at her empty coffee cup, her hair uncombed, her eyes swollen, when she heard—unbelieving—a key in the lock. She felt the cold air as the front door opened. "Aunt Vi, I'm home!" Just like that. The door slammed. She stared. The blur cleared. It really was Ricky. Standing there, grinning. She wanted to fly to him and hug him, but she knew he wouldn't like that. Her grin came slowly and was less dazzling than his. "Well, sit down, man, and I'll fix you a sandwich." And he did. He flopped into his usual chair and asked what Alfy had been doing and how Aunt May was. He was like someone who had been away on vacation.

Patience and punishment. But it didn't work. The school took him back, but it wasn't long before Vi was called back to school. This time he had pulled a knife. He had not made any attempt to use it *("Aw, I was just trying to make him lemmelone"),* but the possibilities of the situation were horrifying. Miss Clewell and Vi talked to him, separately and together, until they were both exhausted. Out of infinite innocence, Ricky maintained that he was just holding the knife for a boy whose name he didn't know.

After Miss Clewell had left, Vi had to say reluctantly, "Rick, I just can't keep you if these things are going to happen. I just can't." And the tears that were in her voice rose to her eyes and spilled out, running in warm little rivers down her face. "I just can't."

He looked up, frightened, his eyes large. "You gon send me away?"

She straightened up, sniffed, wiped her nose on a paper napkin. She was not a woman who cried easily. "Rick, I took you in because I wanted to do you some good. Now, how much good am I doing if you stay in trouble?"

He thought about it. She stood there with her arms folded, not crying now. Finally, he sighed. "I'ma try real hard, Aunt Vi."

And he did, it seemed to Vi. For several weeks there was no serious behavior problem. And he did his chores without complaint. He worked hard at his reading. Miss Clewell was delighted with him. But more than ever, the night fears returned, and each morning he stuffed soggy sheets into the washer.

In spite of his exemplary conduct, Vi had a feeling of foreboding He had lived for so long in the streets, where the only law was the law of survival. The only person who had protected him, given him any love at all, was the charming, troubled father who had ultimately rejected him. There were moments when Vi would glimpse him running down the street with Alfy yipping at his heels, or flopping on the floor in front of the TV or sitting on the front steps with a group of friends, and she would think how really beautiful he was—not thin now but slender, his eyes sparkling with a zest for life.

And suddenly—trouble.

First, Alfy disappeared. Vi got home very late one evening, having worked overtime to finish preparing a case record for Mr. Lassiter, and found Ricky completing his work—mopping the basement—without his jolly little companion. Ricky was whistling.

"Where's Alfy?" Vi had come to love the funny little thing herself, to enjoy his exuberant greeting.

"He gone out. He kept crying at the front door, so I let him go. Musta got him a girl friend." Ricky had turned twelve by now and had begun to suspect that girls had some merit. "He be back."

But he never came back. After dinner they called and searched the streets, fearful that he had been hit by a car. But they never found him, and he never came back. And again love had been snatched away.

A few days later Vi had to be hospitalized. Somehow, she had injured a spinal disk. The pains in her back and legs became so terrible that she finally took a cab to the nearest clinic and eventually found herself in a sterile hospital bed.

Ricky stayed with Johnell for the two weeks during Vi's hospitalization.

"He doing fine," Johnell reported on her first visit, knowing Vi would be worried. "Fit right in with the bunch. You really got him trained good, girl, he just as nice and polite as can be."

Ricky visited every two or three days. Apparently he was enjoying his stay with Johnell. The bed-wetting problem was something of a nuisance, but Johnell's family was understanding "Mr. Joe gon take us to the beach soon as he go on the night shift," Ricky chattered one day, flitting from one subject to another. "And guess what, Mark got a B-B gun, he say he gon let me shoot. And yesterday a real pretty black cat, he came in Miss Johnell's back yard and he ain't had nothing to eat so I give him some lunch meat and he just purred!"

There were no bad incidents at school. Vi began to feel easier in her mind. Miss Clewell dropped in several times to tell her that Ricky was getting along fine, making great progress. At each visit, Ricky chirped merrily on and on about school and Johnell's family and the cat, who showed up daily to be fed and fondled.

When Vi came home she was still bedridden, still not free of pain. Ricky was a big help running errands, fixing sandwiches for her, trying hard to cheer her up. It was the first time he had ever taken care of anybody.

"Man, you something else," Vi said gratefully when he brought her a particularly creative sandwich. "Don't know what I'd do without you." He grinned, and she felt that all the months of struggle had been worth it.

On her third day home Johnell called her, disturbed. She asked the usual things that one asks a sick friend, promised to send dinner that night, then, "Vi, I gotta tell you something—I mean—you gotta know—"

Vi's apprehensions returned, settled around her like an old shawl dropped softly on her shoulders. "What you talking about? What's wrong now?"

"You remember that cat Ricky used to feed when he stayed over my house?"

"Sure—pretty black cat."

"Well, old Mr. Hill—you remember me talking about him—he don't work no more, just sits in his kitchen watching out the window—anyway, Mr. Hill told me he seen the other day—Ricky and a bunch of boys—Ricky was the leader. They got the cat and took it in the lot next to Mr. Hill's window. Vi, *they hung the cat!*"

For a long time after she'd hung up the phone, Vi just sat there, propped up by pillows, surrounded by bottles of pain pills and muscle relaxants and alcohol, her leg throbbing, her throat tight and dry. And now she knew—was beginning to know—the depth of this child's damage. Her mind went back over the months, ferreting out this incident and that, this incongruence and that—his warm response to people and his aversion to being touched, his kindness and his cruelty—and her mind now knew what her heart had felt: that his strange behavior had been, all along, a cry for help.

*Poor boy, to be that desperate, that afraid. Love wasn't enough, patience and punishment wasn't enough. He struggling to become a man, and he never even been a child !* And in her frustration and her pain, finally, she cried.

The next day she called Miss Clewell and told her about the cat. Miss Clewell was shocked. "But I thought Ricky was doing so well! Oh, Mrs. Coleman!"

They agreed that the problems were beyond their skill, that Ricky needed psychiatric help. Miss Clewell promised to make the arrangements right away.

That afternoon she sat at Vi's bedside, her face still furious.

"It doesn't make sense"—she was jabbing her pencil at the air as if it were a knife with which she was cutting her way out of a bag or something. Vi had never seen her angry. Through all their difficulties, she had always kept her cool. But now she was good and mad.

"Of all the stupid things!" She looked so much like an infuriated puppy that even with their trouble, Vi had to smile.

"Miss Clewell, you can cuss if you want to. I won't tell your supervisor. But for the Lord's sake, what happened?"

She lit a cigarette. "I do believe you've got to be sub-human to work at this job. Truly I do. Anyway, I called our medical service to make Ricky's appointment with a psychiatrist. And it was so dumb—I never had to do this before, you know. It was so dumb." She took a long drag.

Vi shifted her position. It hurt. "Well, what happened?"

"I told her that we had a sick child here, and all about the latest thing. So she said the appointments are made through the school and that as soon as school opens, we can see about the appointment."

"Soon as school opens? My Lord, it just finished closing! You mean to say we got to wait the whole summer?"

Miss Clewell smiled grimly. "Not quite. I told her it was an emergency. Went through the whole story again. The result of a whole hour of wheedling and explaining and damn near pulling my hair was—finally—an appointment with a psychiatrist."

"Well, great. When?"

She laughed bitterly. "August 19."

"August 19? Nearly two months! He needs help now!"

She nodded weakly. "That's the way the system works."

"That's the way the system fucks up!" *Don't nobody care about you when you poor and black. The system! That dumb-assed Judge Harmon, giving him to me, just like that. And that stupid bitch wanting to know the dimensions of the room and whether I planned to rape a child. The system! Don't tell me nothing about the system!* "What do we do in the meantime? Suppose next time it's a child instead of a cat."

She whispered, "Then he goes to jail and the law-and-order folks have their day."

They talked for a long time. None of Miss Clewell's courses had prepared her for what it was really like; nothing in her world had told her about the Rickys or the Violas who lived round the corner. And she still couldn't take it all in. She was bewildered even by her own pain.

They decided not to make any changes in Ricky's routine but to encourage him to talk about himself, his feelings, his problems, just a stopgap measure until he was in the hands of a psychiatrist—though deep inside, Vi wondered whether even a psychiatrist could peer into Ricky's world enough to help. But they had to do something.

As Miss Clewell gathered her things to leave, Vi said to herself that it was going to be a long summer.

It was, but for a different reason.

Vi's recovery was slow, and money became scarce. Ricky got two or three jobs of work each week helping people in their yards, scrubbing floors, whatever there was to do. He brought his money home proudly and waited while Vi gratefully gave him back a portion for spending. But things were beginning to go wrong between them. He parried her hints that he talk about himself. He began to stay out later than she thought he should, began to resent her questions about where he spent his time. Irma insisted, "He starting to smell his pee." But Vi found it hard to distinguish between normal stresses of growing up and signs of the invidious damage of all those years of neglect. They had started to get on each other's nerves.

On an airless July night the tension finally exploded.

Vi was able to hobble around the house a little by now but was still forbidden any real exertion. Without a firm routine, she had taken to falling asleep at odd hours. On this night she had fallen asleep after dinner and had awakened after nine to find Ricky gone. Her nervousness mounted for the next two hours. Where was he? What was he into?

She finally heard his key in the lock. This time he didn't call. She met him at the head of the steps. Furious.

"Where you been 'til this time of night?"

"I been out."

"I can see that. Didn't I tell you to be in this house by nine and not to go nowhere without telling me first?"

"You was sleep when I left."

"So where you got to go that's so damn important?"

"I been down the street sitting on the steps with some boys." He was surly now. Mad.

So was she. Her leg was hurting Her patience was at an end. She had done so much for him, and he was repaying her with disobedience and a smart mouth. She knew she was handling him all wrong now, but she couldn't help it. She was so tired, so tired. She went into her room and sat on her bed. He went into his room across the narrow hall and started to close the door.

"Ricky, I don't want you out anywhere at this time of night, you hear me?"

No answer. She could imagine his face, expressionless and dead. Well, damn it, he was going to show her some respect this night.

"Ricky, come in here, I'm talking to you!"

He came and stood in the doorway, towering over her. She began to gather her scattered nerves. Remembering—oh, all there was to remember. His lips were tight, his hands at his sides clenched into fists.

"Look, Rick, you got to understand that you *must* do what I ask you to do." He stood there silent, but his eyes blazed. "Now, you're going to have to go on punishment. You're not to go out for the next week. Not anywhere except to work or to the store. You got to—"

He interrupted with an avalanche of words bringing her down and burying her beneath his rage. "I ain't got to do *nothing*. You think I'm a stay in this house a week? You try and make me—"

"Ricky!"

"You better leave me lone,—" and he cried out incoherent phrases until finally, "I gon beat your ass—"

And she knew that if she let him beat her, she had lost all authority, she had lost him. He reached for his belt. In his fury, his fingers fumbled. She sprang up, wincing with pain from her hurt back, and since she had no weapon but her fists, she balled them up and started at him. "You gon beat whose ass?—"

He dropped his hands and stared at her in confusion. Then he cried out like a hurt animal and dashed past her wildly, over to the open window. In one fluid motion, he tore out the screen and leapt out the window.

Vi screamed and ran to the window. He was rolling off the downstairs awning. As lightly as a leopard, he dropped to the ground, dashed down the street, and was gone.

They found him some weeks later pilfering food from a grocery store. By that time Vi had gathered up his clothes and given them to Miss Clewell.

"It's too much. I can't do it. It's too late. And I'm too old and sick myself."

Miss Clewell had said all the right things—and meant them sincerely. But Vi remained terribly depressed and terribly worried. *You don't stop loving somebody just because you gave up on them. Or because they ain't around. Love ain't got a thing to do with geography.* And besides, she wasn't a person to give up and admit defeat. *But a good run beats a bad stand any old day.* She had reached the end of endurance.

When Miss Clewell called and told her the police had him in Pine Street Station, she was relieved—he was alive, at least. But she refused to have any role in the planning for him from then on. She couldn't help him; he could only destroy her. It was too late.

They sent him back to Boys' Village. Miss Clewell, who had left the Welfare Department by now, visited him now and then as a friend. She called Vi after each contact, told her of Ricky's progress, and invariably concluded, "He asked for you. He wants to see you." Occasionally he would send her a letter, carefully written, copiously misspelled, in which the message was always the same: He wanted to come home; he wanted to see her.

Vi defended herself doggedly against the onslaught of his need. It had been too painful, too damaging, and for all her pain, was he any better off?

She visited him once: There was an autumn open house in which the boys invited their families to meet their teachers and to stay for dinner. Ricky had listed her as his family. She thought of him alone on a day when others would be proudly squiring parents and sisters and brothers. And she couldn't bear the thought. So she went.

He had grown. He was taller than she was now. He was wearing the gold sport coat she had given him last Christmas, but by now his wrists were extending beyond the sleeves. When he saw her, his face lit up in the old happy grin.

He showed her the grounds with the air of a college freshman showing off the campus. He introduced her to his teachers—"This is my aunt"—and glowed when they praised him to her. And she was pleased and proud. He was making progress: for the first time, he was making progress. Dinner was sad because she would soon have to leave.

Goodbyes are always hard. He asked her if she would let him come home: She said he was doing far better here than he had done at home. He asked her if she would come back; she said that she would see.

*It was so hard, so hard.* She wanted to keep it light, not to tear them up. So when the last moment came, she said, "Now, Rick, we not gon cry, because you know, man, when we cry, we *ugly!*"But when she turned to go, he touched her arm—lightly—and she turned around and hugged him hard, and they cried.

She had not seen him since. She had sent him packages and letters, but she could not see him again. He was doing well there. If she visited, if she acted like family, he would plan to come back there after his release, and she just couldn't take him.

Miss Clewell called her a few days before Christmas. "Mrs. Coleman, he'll be practically the only boy who isn't going home for Christmas. Couldn't you take him? It's only for two days."

Vi was in a foul mood, going through all the exhausting rituals of preparing for Christmas, spending money she didn't have. (Alone—alone this year—nobody—) "Miss Clewell, I told him and I told you, it's no use for me to take him, not even for Christmas. After Christmas, it'll be Easter and then weekends, and—no, there's no use to start it. He's got to stop thinking of this house as home."

"But it's Christmas, and he's got no place to go."

"Then why don't you take him?" That was cruel, she knew. But she had to end this discussion before she weakened.

On Christmas Eve they called her from Boys' Village to ask if she had heard from Ricky. He had run away.

For moments after the voice had silenced, she sat there at the kitchen table still holding the phone to her ear until the insistent beep-beep filtered through the holes in her thoughts. She hung up and stared blindly at the naked wall, thinking without words, thinking with some instinctive faculty deep inside. She leaned wearily on her elbows and closed her eyes, cupping her cheek in her hand. The radio was still shrieking between commercials, "Tis the season to be jolly," but she heard neither that nor the cacophony of the traffic outside, nor the loud ticking of the clock, nor anything. She sat there while time flowed by, sat there and felt the rhythms of her life, the currents that had swept her to this time and this place. *Ricky...Ricky... Out there in the cold without even a coat that fits....What's he into now? Is he hungry?*

Without words her inner self groped for patterns in the chaos of her life, the absurdity of her aloneness, the depth of her need and Ricky's. Big Ma, Aunt May, even Stick—all the years and all the people that were her self crowded into her thought and floated into the collage of her contemplation. Ricky's mother deteriorating in a mental hospital, his father's genial and lethargic desperation, the poverty that called the tune to which they all danced, the hatred that every Black child takes in with its mother's milk.

And now she knew—with the wisdom of her dark fathers and mothers, she knew—not only the fact of the omnipotent System which manipulated them all, but also the pervasive cruelty of that System, which counted Black lives as nothing, Black suffering as inconsequential, Black humanity as nonexistent; which would cut down Black manhood and womanhood lest they become the pebble that clogs the machinery of the Great White Way. She knew that, with greater clarity than she had ever known it before.

But she knew something else, too: that she, Viola Coleman, had held in her hand the power to create changes, little changes, but then maybe bigger than that. Yes, she, Vi, had the power to shape a destiny, Ricky's destiny, to undo the damage done to one small person, to (maybe) reshape his destiny or help him reshape his own destiny—a little—but a little is a damn sight better than none. (And Stick? Maybe if just one of them had understood—?) And now, had she lost the chance? Would Ricky come to her, or was he running from her? O God, the streets—vicious—murderous. He had teetered between complete loss and at least partial salvage, and she had pushed him from her for the sake of her peace of mind—which could never be more than illusory. Murderous streets. Vile.

But if he came to her, then what? Half-grown now—could really beat her ass if he chose. Psychiatrist? Would a clean-fingered white man really understand? What? Scattered thoughts, falling like autumn leaves.

But could she find a way? Yes, he had improved this time; there was a spark of hope. Oh, but she wasn't strong, wasn't infallible! But then—why, she wasn't alone either. Aunt May, Johnell, even Irma, maybe even—Stick. And Ricky himself. The survival instinct. Yes, there was power. There was power.

Christmas. White folks' sacred day, and they have made it unclean. They had made the whole world unclean. And Vi's fear became anger, became rage that infused every fiber of her body and would never, in all her life, entirely leave her. And that rage, that too was power.

Christmas. She thought way back to the rickety frame church in Virginia and the long-legged black man whose fiery words and fearful images had taught them the way and prayed them out of all the hate and destruction the white folks could throw at them. The Christmases when you got an orange and a few nuts in your stocking and maybe a homemade toy and were happy, because the kinfolks and neighbors came around and everything was so warm and funny and good, yes my Lord. And they had sung in church—she now found herself humming softly—"Sweet little Jesus boy—."

In the warmth of her memory, Ricky's face came back to her, his sparkling eyes and quick smile. And remembering his awful desperation and her turning him away, remembering the kitten that she had let die because she was afraid of white folks' opinions, and knowing that Ricky was out in the December cold because she had not loved enough— remembering all these things, she cried.

---

Now the Christmas company has gone, and she sits alone, the meaningless ritual of Christmas Eve completed. The familiar room is strange, bizarre in the lurid shifting shadows of the blinking lights. Her life is like a warped recording of "O Come All Ye Faithful." *Ricky—Where did you run to? It's cold out, and nowadays people lock their cars.* He had touched her arm that day at open house, had let her hug him. Was struggling so hard to become whole. But who can struggle alone? Those who must. *I was wrong. Ricky Where did you run to? I was wrong.*

She gets up. Blows her nose on a Christmas napkin. Slowly wipes away the tears.

She does not believe the sound at first. A key in the lock. *Oh Lord, I thought he'd lost it—after all this time!* She stands still as the shifting shadows pelt her like snowflakes. The door opens quietly.

"Aunt Vi— " softly, then louder—"Aunt Vi—I'm home." And again, with joy, "I'm home!"

# Breeder

*Children, I been'buked and I been scorned.*

African American Spiritual

And when Aunt Peggy spoke, this is what she said: I reckon I never told you much about my life because remembering hurt so bad. And because I figured you was too young to understand. You's still too young, but I guess I ain't got much more time to wait. It's dreadful to pass out'n this world without nobody know about you. Seem like after you dead, maybe a little bit of you is still alive if there's somebody that know about you. So I reckon it's time for me to talk some about all them years behind me. And you, child, you's all the family I got. Anyways, one of these days you might meet up with my Frederick, and I wants you to tell him about his mama. Yes, you'll know him. Ain't many people with just one foot. I'll tell you about that. Just be quiet now and listen. And remember—even what you cain't understand now, remember. And pass it on.

I was born in South Carolina, Laurens County. Try to remember that—Laurens County. My massa was a rich man, name of Willard Price. Say that name now—Willard Price—Laurens County—good. Cause if you does meet up with Frederick, he'll know you talking about me. It was a great big plantation, many head of slaves.

I don't recollect too much about my mama. She was a field hand, and time she got in from the field I had done fell asleep, and she carried me sleep to our cabin. All us children, we was watched over by a old woman whilst our mamas worked in the field. She so old, she slept mostly, and we done most anything we was big enough to do. Hah! Run around naked or nigh to it while that old woman nodded in a chair in the doorway. When the sun got high, one of the slaves from the big house brought a tub of vittles and poured it into a trough. All us children and the old granny, too, would sit around the trough and dip in our hands and eat fast as we could, cause who didn't eat *fast* didn't eat *much*. Then we played 'til we like to drop, and our mamas pick us up and carry us to the cabins. So I don't recollect much about my mama. She was a tall woman, black-black. Strong. I never did know my daddy.

On Sundays my mama didn't have to go to the field. The people would sit around the cabins and talk, rest a little from they labors. Some would tend they little vegetable patches the massa let them keep. We'd have service out in the field sometimes or in the hush-harbor, whenever the preacher could come. Nighttime we'd kinda drift together again and folks would sing. Oh, that was the best time. Them songs, child—I was too young to know in my head what they meant to them people, but deep inside myself I could feel that it was them singing times that kept everybody going. I could feel it. Somehow everybody seemed to be kin. I'd get up in my mama's lap and I'd feel her body swaying or her feet tapping or something. She would close her eyes, and I would feel her sorrow and her joy. You think *I* can sing? Girl, you shoulda heard my mama. Oh, you shoulda heard her. Wait a minute, Caroline—

Well—I don't remember much about them days. I
was so young, just a weeny mite. But I remembers at
night curling up around my mama on the pallet and
feeling warm and good. I remembers dropping off to
sleep with her arms around me and her breathing
soft like a lullaby. But sometimes she'd cry and hug
me fit to break my ribs. I didn't know why then. But
I knows now. Anyway, seem like before we got asleep
good, that horn would be blowing again for
everybody to get up and I'd be back with the old
granny and the other slave children.

I remembers well that dreadful morning when
my mama got sold. Child, many's the time I wished I
could forget it, but I couldn't. And then I didn't want
to forget it, cause it's almost all I got of my mama.
And even something that hurts you so bad, if it's all
you got, you holds to it tight.

Everybody knowed that the scroungy looking
white man that came to see Massa was a slave
trader. Even me, and I wasn't no more than four-five
summers. But the folks in the quarters all knowed
that the slave trader had been in to see Massa.

"Massa been gambling heavy," the old cook
whispered. Course, I didn't know what gambling was.

"Crops wasn't too good this year," said a field
hand.

"I heard Massa tell Missy them folks up North
ain't paying nothing for tobaccy,"said the coachman.

"Some us gonna git sold!" The awful word went
round and round the quarters. Some people cried.
Some prayed. Some just carried on. Nobody knowed
who would be sold or when. The old people just sat
and looked, cause they knowed didn't nobody want
them. But some had children, and they was scairt,
too. People would stop in our cabin at night and say
to my mama, "If it's me, take care of my Francie" or
"If it's me, look out for my old papa."

And when she went to the field every day, my mama looked at me hard like she didn't want to leave me. And all us children cried when our mamas went to the field, though we didn't know why. But days went by and nothing happened, so by and by us children went to running in the sun like we always done.

One Sunday morning they come. The white men. The slave trader's men. We hear them tramping through the quarters. My mama grab me and her arms is hard, hard. She crouch in the darkest corner of our cabin, holding on to me and praying to the Lord to spare us. We hear the men stop at a cabin just up the way and call, "Annie—Annie! That girl Annie, come out!" And we hear sobs and the clink of chains. My mama stop praying and listen. She look all around like a rabbit I once seen cornered by dogs. But the only way out was the door, and the white men was out there. We hear wailing all over the quarters.

Next cabin. "Josiah! Josiah—git moving, nigger!" Uncle Josiah was nowheres near young, but he could read and even figger. We hear his wife, Aunt Daisy, scream. We hear a scuffle. "You better git back, old woman. I know you don't want none of this whip!" The clink of chains. And old Uncle Josiah crying.

The sunlight in the doorway broke up by that white man.

Outside we seen Miss Annie and Uncle Josiah and two three others chained together, crying and moaning And we seen them white men swinging they whips. The white man in the doorway was bigger than anything ever I seen before. And red-face, arms all red with white hairs all over the arms. Funny the things you remember, ain't it? Yellow hair, eyes blue like fish eyes. Big. Bigger than anything in the world. He was looking at a piece of paper.

"Mary—girl name Mary here?" The sun done blinded his eyes and he didn't see us right away. "Where Mary?"

My mama held onto me like the grip of death. Her body felt cold like ice. She wasn't hardly breathing. The big white man come on into the cabin, nigh stumbled over a stool, cussed. Then seen us. "Didn't you hear me calling you? Git on out here, gal!"

My mama screamed. I never heard nothing like it before nor since, less'n it be my own screams when they took my own little children. She hollered loud and long like something not of this here earth. The white man grabbed hold of her arm and jerked her up, but she held on to me with both arms.

"That pickaninny don't go! Now set it down!"

We was both screaming by now, and I still remember the dreadful fear, hot like boiling water, because I didn't know before then that they was taking my mama away. My mama held onto me and kicked that white man and tried to bite him. That big white man balled up his fist and hit my mama in the face and in the stomach, and some of them licks fell on me, but I didn't feel nothing, I was screaming so. And finally he kicked her legs and knocked her down on the ground and kicked her hard in the head and her arms got all loose. I tried to hold on to her, but I wasn't strong enough. The white man pulled her and when I tried to come after her, he kicked me down. I remember crawling to the cabin door. And when I got outside I seen my mama chained with Uncle Josiah and Miss Annie and them, dragged out of the quarters in them heavy chains.

We followed along, crying and wailing, all of us, and they tried to reach out to us but they couldn't 'cause their hands was chained. They looked back at us and cried. Oh child, child, I cain't never forget it. Aunt Sally's boy was amongst them, boy about thirteen-fourteen. He kept calling to her, "Mama, don't you worry, I gon be a good boy. Don't you cry, Mama!" And Lindie's man—they'd done jumped the broom not two full moons ago—he kept yelling, "Lindie—I coming back to you—I coming back—" And my mama just kept crying my name— "Peggy—Peggy—Peggy—" Oh, child. And we followed them to the end of the plantation, crying and screaming, until the white men beat us back with they whips, and all we could see of our people was dust in the road.

Scuse me, child. Old Aunt Peggy ain't shed a tear for many a day. Just a minute....

Well, I growed up on that plantation. Different folks took care of me til I got big enough to take care of myself. Many's the things I seen in them growing-up years, child. Many's the things. We in the quarters was like a family—a family held together by sorrow. Our own blood families was busted so bad we couldn't hardly think on them. There was men who wouldn't have wives on the same plantation 'cause they couldn't bear to sit by helpless and watch they women git beat and 'bused. There was men who cussed the day they become fathers 'cause they couldn't bear to see they children treated bad and sold away. There was women who wouldn't never see they men again and was liable to any white man's lust, will it or no. And there was children who never knowed they ma and pa, and folks whose children was gone forever. It was a time, child, it was a time.

So we was a family. When anybody died or got sold away, it was all our loss, and anybody's trouble belonged to us all. And if anybody runned away, we was all glad. I don't know how it was nowhere else, but that's how it was with us. Sure, there was plenty fusses, and some didn't git along with others. Some folks just stayed to theyself and did they work and waited to die,' cause they done took all they could. But we was still a family. 'Cause we didn't have nothin but each other.

Well, the years went running by fast as a stream in springtime. Though they seemed slow to me then. I couldn't hardly wait to grow up so's I could run off from there, head north where they told me freedom was. It was a scary thing, running off. But I was determined to go, soon's I got big and strong enough. If I'd a knowed that evil old Massa's plans for me, I'd a went anyways, big enough or no.

I growed into a right comely gal, tall and straight, strong from working all them years in the field. And I soon come into my womanhood. You'll know all about that 'fore long. And I started thinking real serious about taking off from there.

But one day while we was turning the soil for the new crop, Massa come riding that big white horse of his'n right out to the field where we was. Old devil! He rid up and down awhile, looking at us right careful. The old man who always led the singing, he switched us from the work song that helped us dig to "Walk Together." You know that one. "Walk together, children, don't you git weary, there's a big camp meeting in town tonight." What he was saying was, everybody look careful and listen well to see what Massa is up to, and we can talk about it later.

Massa looked a long time, then started saying something to the overseer. They looking over where I was working. Then he point his riding stick right at me. I got kinda weak all over, but I kept singing with the others. I figured Massa was choosing somebody to sell. The overseer grinned kinda strange and nodded his head. I kept on working, but my hands was trembling so bad I couldn't hardly hold the shovel, and my knees was so weak that I like to fell.

Caroline, them next days was awful days. I was scairt of every shadow, every sound. I kept remembering them quiet days before my mama got sold and that dreadful day they took her from me, and that made me wonder some more where she was and whether she was still alive and whether she still thought about me. I was in a awful state. I didn't want to be sold. Bad as it was there, it was all I knowed. I wanted to run away to freedom, not to be sold to harder slavery. Them girls I shared a cabin with, girls like me with no folks or nothing, they tried to cheer me up, but I's nervous as a sparrow.

Then one morning when I goes to the field with the others, that old overseer point his whip at me, say, "Peggy, massa say for you to go up to the big house." I felt like a tree had done fell on me. I just stood there, staring like somebody gone fool. 'Til I heared that redfaced old white man hollering, "What I say? Now, git." I musta looked so funny, he sent Big Jerome up to the house with me. Big Jerome so big and dumb, he do everything them white folks tells him, and I didn't stand no chance of running away.

We goes in the back door. Massa and Missy theyself waiting for me in the summer kitchen. When they sees me they grins at each other and looks me all over and says to each other yes, this'n do fine, good strong stock. I so scairt I cain't find no voice to ask what I'm s'posen to do. They tells Big Jerome take me to the empty cabin by the buttonwood tree and leave me there.

I sits in that cabin, on the floor right by the door, 'plexed and troubled, not knowing what in the world to do. Before I could make a right good plan, the door open and this big black man come in. Great big man, full-bearded, big-muscled like somebody done worked in the sun all his life. I thought he must be the slave trader's man. He seen me sitting on that floor staring at him, scairt to death, and he stared back at me.

74

"Lawd," he say after a while, "What they 'spect me to do with this here child?"

"I stood up, ready to run out that door if I could just git a chance. He seen I was scairt and he just stood there, put them big hands on his hips and laughed—kinda strange, like wasn't nothing really funny. "What's wrong with you, gal? Ain't none of these here boys got to you yet?" I was beginning to know what he was there for. I seen what roosters do to chickens and bulls do to cows. And I had heard that some massas bred slaves like cattle. I was flat against the wall, inching away from him. He start to unroll the pallet somebody had left, over by the corner. I starts for the door, but he grab my arm and pull me over to him. He hold on to my shoulders.

"You think I like this kinda work? Well maybe— sometimes. But you just a child." He slacken his grip, and I starts for the door again. He grab me. "Look— set down here, dammit." He laugh again, like there still ain't nothing funny. "You ain't got nothing I ain't seen before."

Caroline, I ain't gon tell you all what happened in that cabin. It ain't time yet for you to know such things. There's things that's supposed to happen to a young girl, but not like that, not when she's too young to feel nothing but hurt and shame, and not when she git used like a animal in the bushes. Worse. 'Cause a dog don't use a bitch when she ain't in heat. We stayed together many days, that man and me, and after he left and went back to his massa, they let me live in that cabin. And in time I got big with the child growing in me, a child—something at last that was mine, mine.

My baby girl was born just before Christmas. It weren't easy. You gon know that pain yourself, Caroline. But finally my baby was born. Strong, healthy girl. I named her Mary, after my mama. Dark like my mama, and I sort of thought she looked like my mama, too. The old folks say the spirit of the dead come back in newborn babies, and I wondered about that. She looked so like I remembered my mama. So I named her Mary.

She growed real nice. I took her to the field on my back. And she was the only thing in all this world that was really mine. Mine. After awhile she was too big to carry to the field, so I had to leave her with old Aunt Daisy along with the other little 'uns. And carried her sleep to our cabin after sundown, and curled around her at night, loving her so hard and fearing so terrible.

And one day they come and took her. And sold her to the slave trader. I ain't gon talk about that. I cain't, even now. My Mary. I named her after my mama. They took her. They took her.

Child, you cain't never be again what you once was. When you done lost something, you cain't never git back to the time before you had it. Not if it ever meant something to you. They took my Mary. My baby girl.

Anyways—it wasn't long before the overseer told me again—"Don't come to the field today, Peggy. Go on home to your cabin." And I knowed what they wanted.

Well, I didn't go back to no cabin. I wasn't no old sow they could make have little pigs for them white folks to eat. I run down by the pasture thinking to cut through the trees and over the fence. I didn't care where I went after that, I didn't even care if the pattyrollers got me and killed me. But one of the nigger-drivers caught me before I could get over. Oh, child, I fought him, I fought so hard. And I was so strong he couldn't do much with me. Then the other driver he come along and hit me back of my head with something. I didn't know nothing else 'til I come to myself in the cabin. And sure enough, they had done sent a man in there. And I didn't have no choice.

This time I prayed for the child to die in my belly. I done everything I knowed to make it die, but it kept a-growing. The bigger it growed the sadder I got, and the first time I felt it move I cried like I'd done felt death moving inside me. I swore I'd never let myself love this'n. 'Cause I knowed now that it weren't none of mine, it belonged to them white folks. As my time got near, I prayed so hard it would die a-borning. Well, that didn't happen. This time the birth come easy, and soon's I heared that loud cry, I knowed the baby was fine and healthy. And I knowed I loved it.

And I knowed what I had to do. I turned my face to the wall, and tears run down my face like a waterfall. I had to do what young Sairy, two cabins down, done for her'n. I had to kill it. I had to kill my little baby. Out of love, child. I had to kill out of love. So when Bella the midwife brought me my baby I wouldn't even look at it, just held it loose-like and wouldn't look at it. Bella stood there awhile—she'd done brought out so many slave women's babies, I think she knowed what I had in mind. She just stroked my hand a minute, then went on away.

Finally, I looked down at my little baby sleeping so sound, wrapped in a soft piece of cloth. I laid it down easy and felt for some rags down there beside the pallet. I knowed what I had to do. Out of love. I spread them rags over that little face and pressed down hard, hard, pressed out all the air I could. And the baby it tried to cry out under that rag and jerked its little arms. Oh, child, it ain't nature to destroy what you done created. It ain't nature to kill out of love. I didn't have the strength to do it. I knowed I ought to, but I didn't have the strength. I jerked them rags off my baby's face and I held her warm in my arms until the fear left her and she slept. But the fear didn't leave me, and I didn't sleep. I cried and cried until the morning light and then I laid there holding my new baby girl and feeling like the Lord hisself had done deserted me.

Jane was a nice little girl, real bright, and from the first, try so hard to please me. When she was two, they sent me home from the fields again. And this time I couldn't try to run away because I couldn't leave my Jane. The man didn't want to be there no more'n me. But he said if he didn't produce he liable to be sold, and he had a woman and children on his own plantation, so he didn't have no say-so. We done in sadness what men and women is supposed to do in joy.

The baby was a boy, born too soon and like to died. But the call to life is so strong, child, I prayed for him to live and he did. Jane and Benjy was my life. Benjy being born too soon, Massa musta thought I wasn't no more good for bearing, 'cause he didn't send me from the field no more. And when the years went by and Massa didn't sell my children, I got to hoping we would always be together, thinking I really had something of my own.

I always remembered my Mary. Every Christmas when the slaves had they day off and drink they pint of whiskey Massa give them, I kept thinking, my Mary must be six year old now, or my Mary seven now, wonder is she well and treated good, or my Mary nine year old, wonder do she ever think about her mama.

The plantation begun to fail. Sure we know it. Down in the quarters, we know. The cook and coachman, they tell us a lot. Them house niggers what lives with Massa and Missy, they just like white folks, we don't even know them. But cook and coachman, they lives with us, and they tells us what goes on. And Massa gitting deeper and deeper in debt. His children growed up and making all kinds of trouble. Young Missy Helen, she about to get married, and we knows what that mean: big parties and balls and a big wedding. Money. And we know Massa ain't got that much money. So we know he gon sell some of us, like he always done.

I cain't tell you about it. The memory still burns like it was yestiddy. They took my Jane and my Benjy. She was seven, he not even five. They took them. Spite of all our fighting and screaming. 'Cause that was what they was born for. Bred for. In that cabin with them strange men I never seen before nor since.

And when it was over, when my children was gone and I had done screamed 'til I didn't have no voice and I had done cried 'til my eyes couldn't make no more water, I sat crouched by they empty pallet and I listened. And I didn't hear nothing at all. And that nothing was the loudest thing I ever heared in my whole life. I sat crouched there in all that emptiness and I thought I was the only person left in the world. Then I heared a voice singing right outside my cabin. It was old Sal, the cook, who had seen so many folks come and go. Old Sal singing:

> *Soon one morning death come creepin in my room.*
> *Soon one morning death come creepin in my room.*
> *Soon one morning death come creepin in my room.*
> *O my Lawd! O my Lawdy, what shall I do?*

And then somebody else started singing with her, a man with a low, heavy voice. And then somebody else. I got up and went on outside, too. And soon most everybody in the quarters was out there singing them old songs that everybody knowed. 'Cause them folks who hadn't lost nobody this time still could remember when they did, and besides that, we was a family, and anybody's loss was everybody's loss. So we sat together and sung away the night, sung away the hurt until we could bear another sunrise.

Them next years I didn't care whether I lived or died. I worked in the fields, then came back to that empty cabin and slept. I et just enough to keep my stomach from crying too loud. I looked like a sack of bones.

But, child, life reaches out to life, will it or no. We commence to hear about how slaves is escaping north and how a woman name Moses is taking folks away from slavery and how white folks theyself is arguing over slavery. And them songs we sings is used to tell people how to escape to freedom. The old preacher man what come to us every three-four Sundays, he tell us these things. He was a free man. He go from one plantation to the next, and after the sermon, he gather the news and tell us what he done learned from the others. And we knows a lot what is going on. After awhile I comes alive again. Child, life is mighty hard to stamp out.

After awhile I gits to liking a man. His name Jerdan, and he was a boy I growed up with. Kinda skinny, never big and strong like the field hands. But he was smart, so Massa let him help in the commissary. He had a wife and child in the quarters, but they both died of sickness the same winter. Anyways, Jerdan had done lost so much and I had done lost so much, we kinda reached out to each other, and after awhile we both wanted to be together all the time.

Spite of all the hard work and trouble, I felt like my whole life was shiny and new like a April morning. Before Jerdan, I figgered I was just a brood mare, fit for nothing but stallions. But Jerdan taught me things about myself that I never knowed before. Child, if I done lived this long, it's mostly 'cause I had that time with Jerdan. A woman need a man for her completion, just like a man need a woman. And I found my completion in Jerdan.

No, he wasn't sold away. Jerdan died. One winter, round about our fifth winter together, everything was scarce, food, firewood, warm clothes, everything. By February most of the slaves was down with fever. Me and Jerdan both come down with it, but Jerdan, seem like he couldn't get over his'n. By the middle of March, he had done closed his eyes forever. But this time I wasn't alone. 'Cause inside me I had Jerdan's child.

Well, them was terrible days. I wasn't gon let nobody take this'n from me. I went to the hoodoo woman, got me a charm to keep my child. But I's scairt that weren't enough—hoodoo don't always work on white folks. So I thought and worried and prayed the child would be too scrawny to sell. One early morning at harvest time, my Frederick was borned.

Big baby, fat, pretty as could be. Brown as a little chestnut. Friendly and happy almost from the beginning. And I knowed that there wasn't nothing I wouldn't do to keep my child. Nothing. And I knowed that when he got big enough, Massa would just as soon sell him as not.

The answer came to me in the dead of the night. Just like the voice of Jesus hisself. If the child was cripple, wouldn't nobody buy him! I looked down on my little baby, perfect and strong, and I knowed what I had to do.

I couldn't do it right away. It was dreadful to think on. But the memory of my Mary and my Benjy and my Jane give me strength. So that next Sunday I carried my baby into the woods beyond the meadow. I took along a old meat cleaver that Jerdan had done brought from the big house years before. I laid Frederick down and sharpened the blade on a rough stone, sharpened it as best I could, then wiped it clean on some leaves. My baby was sleeping so quiet. I was trembling so bad I most couldn't do it.

But I kept hearing the cries of my other babies when they was tore from me to be sold, kept seeing they faces all twisted up and they eyes—oh! And I prayed to the Lord to guide my hand.

I found a piece of tree branch just the right size. Frederick sleeping so good he didn't rouse when I bent his knee and set his little foot on top that branch. I raised that cleaver and prayed not to miss. And with all my strength, I swung that blade down, down through the foot and branch, down into the ground. That sound echo in my head always. And the awful sound of my little baby's cries—and child, the sight of that poor little foot cut clean off, all but the heel and ankles. The blood—oh, child, child—I'll carry that memory to my grave.

But it worked. Massa couldn't sell Frederick, though he did sell some of the people. I always said a animal in the woods had bit Frederick's foot off, and Massa so dumb as to believe it. But the slaves, they knowed. Frederick and me, we managed tolerable well. He learned to walk with a stick and sometimes limped along without no stick at all. Seeing as how he couldn't do no heavy field work, Massa put him to work in the house, and everything he saw and heard there, Frederick came back and told us. He was a good boy, happy and loving to everybody.

He was about ten when the war come. Seem like the whole world had went crazy. Lots of the men on our plantation run off to join the Yankees, and by and by there wasn't enough left to work the fields. Massa and Missy tried to keep up the old ways like nothing wasn't happening, but after a while they musta looked foolish even to theyself. They started going around all confused like pigs in a horse stable. Then the gov'ment come and took the horses and whatever we had. But we was rejoicing before the Lord because we knowed the day of Jubilee was finally come.

When the men commence to leave, I know Frederick want to go, too. And after awhile he did. I wanted to go with him, but he say no, he gon find the Yankees and git into the war. I weren't young no more and going through a sickly time. So Frederick say, "You stay here, Mama. I coming back to git you after we's free."

So we said goodby to one another late one night.

He was just old enough for his voice to start going deep. But my Frederick, he was a man!

And the last time I seen my Frederick he was a shadow slipping up the road in the moonlight, hobbling on his stick, heading for freedom.

Well, I stayed there, me and some of the old folks. And I watched that place crumble. When the Yankees come, everybody else followed them. Contrabands, they was called. The war ended, and still Frederick didn't come. Most of the old folks had done died long since, with nobody but me to close they eyes. I knowed that if I stayed there any longer I would die along with that plantation. Massa and Missy theyself walked around like nervous ghosts.

So one day in early spring, when the leaves is tender and the grass just starting to green, I gathers up what little things I has, and I starts out, going north to find my Frederick. My other children—I give up hope of seeing them ever again. If they still living, I wouldn't know them, and they wouldn't know me. In my heart they's still my babies, but by now they's growed, maybe even named different and done forgot they ma. But Frederick—he north somewheres, and I know him forever, cause he ain't got but one foot.

Many's the road I traveled, and many's the things I seen. Frightful things, child. Black bodies rotting in the sun, all swelled up and foul. Houses burnt out, fields destroyed. Old folks and children with no place to go and nobody to see to them. White

faces twisted with hate. And Ku Kluxers with them
sheets over them, riding into the night. I seen some
things. But I moved steady northward, working
when I could, asking everybody if they seen a black
man with one foot. 'Cause, child, once you love
somebody—love somebody deep down inside
yourself, you cain't never, ever stop.

Well, by the time I got here, I was old and tired.
And now I ain't got no time left. So I gon have to
stay, and I done give up hope of seeing my Frederick
this side of the grave. But, child, you's got a long life
yet. And Frederick is still living—somewhere. If he'd
a died, I'd know it; something inside me woulda told
me. Maybe he's somewhere looking for his ma.
Anyways, if you sees a black man with no right
foot—he be in the prime of his manhood about
now—ask him if his name be Frederick and tell him
about me. Tell him how hard I looked for him and
how I never stopped loving him, not for a single
second.

I done talked for so long, I right tired now. And
the half ain't yet been told. You here, where there
ain't no black folks but me to tell you who you is. You
ain't my born child, but you's my child anyways. I
ain't got nothing to leave you but my life. And now I
done give that to you as best I knows how.

Pass it on, child. When the time comes, pass it
on.

# Rachel's Children

I am jotting these notes as a means of sorting
things out. Even the maddest things somehow
make sense when they are codified into words and
sentences with periods and semi-colons and things.
The events of these past months have become jumbled
in my mind, and I am left with a pervasive dread
which colors my days. Perhaps if I try to write them
all out, as I used to do in college when my world was
suddenly a riddle, I can make sense out of what has
happened; perhaps I can quiet these awful, irrational
thoughts.

For I am terribly, terribly afraid that I am losing
my mind.

It seems to me now that I should have had some
sense of foreboding when I first saw this house. But
I had none. A cheery real estate agent, a sunny
morning with all the heady perfume of a southern
April—they can charm away the most persistent of
hovering spirits, at least temporarily. Now, in this
disturbing time, I believe—*I actually believe*—that I
was somehow meant to be the one to buy this
property, that some force drew me, via Sloan and
Carter Realtors, to this house and compelled me to
buy it. But that is one of those irrational thoughts
that I must face and purge.

I bought this house because it was adequate and
because it was cheap. And because it was reasonably

close to the college where I would be teaching in the
fall. All sensible reasons. I remember how amazed I
was at my own daring, pulling up stakes after all
those years in D.C. and going south alone to wind up
my teaching career in a small Black college! Well,
that was an old dream, begun in graduate school
before the teaching and writing and lecturing, back
when Edward and I were young history majors in
Dr. Hansberry's class, before the marriage and the
hard years and the boys and the better years—and
now my Edward, my Edward is gone!

But I am rambling again.

Certainly the house looked most unlikely when I
first saw it. As we drove up a winding country road
toward the summit of a hill, there was the house set
back a bit on the right side of the road. It looked like
a New England salt box house misplaced in the deep
South. The white paint had long since greyed, and
much of it had peeled off, leaving bare dry planks.
But the windows were still intact, and
incongruously, the front door had in its center an
elaborate carving of a noonday sun. At least it looked
to me like a noonday sun. The rooms inside were
much better kept than the outside would indicate.
The agent—what was her name?—Miss Simpson or
somebody, who looked as if Mummy and Daddy were
proudly smiling that their darling had gotten this
nice job selling these lovely old houses. Anyway, the
agent explained that the owner used the place only a
few weeks in the fall for a hunting lodge, when he
and his friends came to shoot deer in the woods just
beyond. The house seemed basically sound, with
modern plumbing and sturdy walls. If the frame was
unaesthetic and the grounds overgrown with weeds
and poorly landscaped, those things could be fixed. It
began to feel like a good deal.

The house was younger than the rest of the
estate. It had been built around the turn of the

century and later renovated two or three times over. Apparently there had been another house on the premises—the "big house" in slave parlance—but Miss What's-her-name didn't know what had happened to it. The property was quite extensive considering the price. There were a number of crumbling out-buildings, some of which probably did date back to antebellum days. The property was ringed by woods on three sides. There was, surprisingly, a pond with lily pads and even a family of ducks. It was the pond that sold me. I bought the property.

But no, I think that the real reason I bought this house was that it appealed to my sense of history. For two centuries this was slave territory, here in the deep South, where generations of Black people toiled and suffered and somehow survived on the distant hope of freedom. That was my specialty, Black American history, but for me the research and teaching have been more than a job—they have something to do with a sense of who I am and who my sons are. Standing on earth which was once part of an actual plantation (as the bubbly little red-headed agent joyously informed me), I did feel a tug toward buying it. There seemed a sort of poetic justice in the property's ending up in the hands of a Black woman, to be handed down to her generations. Certainly my people had earned it.

I moved south with all kinds of trepidation. My friends told me it was too soon for me to make a major decision. But Edward had been gone for more than a year, and the old life had become meaningless. I kept seeing vestiges of Edward everywhere, taunting me with what I had had and could never have again. Then, too, I was born in the South, and after upheaval, you feel a primal urge to return to your roots.

Kenneth and David, I think, were relieved to see me starting a new life without them. They had been shocked and grieved over their father's death, and had come with their wives and children to pay their respects and offer me their love and support. *(Ken and Davie, fathers!)* But grown sons have their own lives, and after that first Thanksgiving in Cleveland with Kenneth's family, and then Christmas in Los Angeles with David's, I knew that I needed to build a life of my own, and that's when I revived our old dream, Edward's and mine, to go south and teach in some small Black college. Between the insurance money and the sale of the Washington house—and having nobody, nobody but myself to provide for—I knew I could manage on the smaller salary.

But the unknown is always fearful, and as I drove south to meet the movers at my new home, I was afraid.

By then the exterior of the house had been repaired and painted a sparkling white. The grass had been cut, the wild vines and bushes removed, and something of the old splendor restored. The carved sun on the front door gleamed brilliantly, and my fears began to fade. As I stepped out of the car and stood looking at my new home, for a moment I felt a marvelous sense of a bright beginning. No foreboding. *O God!*

The children came first by two's and three's. They stood there by the road watching silently as the movers unloaded the van. Black children, white children, some holding the hands of younger children or standing arm in arm with special pals. They were shy but friendly, rushing to pick up things I dropped and generally supervising from a distance. I had the feeling that my yard had been their running space, especially after the tall weeds had been cut, and that they were checking out the new owner with some anxiety. By now I was experiencing

some anxiety again myself, wondering what insanity
had prompted me to leave my accustomed routine
and to journey forth into aloneness. Somewhere
along the line, I paused and grinned at them. "My
name is Jennifer Watts. Do you live around here?"

They smiled back and collectively muttered
something. One thin brown little girl seemed to
speak for them. "We live in the projects over there."
She waved her hand in the direction across the road
and down the hill. We play here sometimes."

"Well, come back and see me." I was struggling
with a heavy suitcase. A little boy offered to help,
but he didn't seem any stronger than I. So I thanked
him and said I could manage, and when I came back
outside sometime later, they were gone.

Somewhere during that first restless night, they
drifted back into my thoughts, and the image of the
thin little girl emerged from all the rest. Shy smile,
bright darting eyes, thin arms gesturing—and
something—something about her that made you
remember.

Helen.

What was there about those children that I
found troubling?

Next morning when I ventured outside to look
things over (reflecting that I really must see about
putting up porches), they were there, four of them,
lolling in front of some old azalea bushes and,
apparently, waiting uncertainly for my appearance.

"Good morning," I called, glad for someone to
talk to. I had awakened with a strange feeling that I
had had fearful forgotten dreams which had left me
with an intangible unease.

They scampered over. "Morning, Miz—" They
had forgotten my name.

"Watts. Jennifer Watts."

"Morning, Miz Jenny." (So much for Dr. Watts, I smiled to myself, thinking that I would much rather be Miz Jenny).

"And what are your names?"

"Me, I'm Helen," said the little girl who had so impressed me the day before. The chubby white boy, around ten, was Robert, and the light-skinned little Black girl with the two thick braids was Catherine. The handsome boy, seven or so, with curly black hair and smooth skin the color of maple bark, was Brian. They were my self-appointed escorts in exploring my new environment. The vestiges of my troubled dreams melted away as we went scurrying over the dry grass to see what was where.

I do love children. Even when my Edward was with me (my Edward!), I missed the presence of children after Ken and Davie grew up.

First, we looked over the outbuildings near the house. They were all old and rotted and should have been demolished long ago. There was something that had apparently been a storage building for farm equipment. There was an open shed, used for heaven knows what. There was—would you believe it?—an old outdoor toilet, with splintered seats and (did I imagine it?) lingering odors from long-ago droppings. We stopped at the duck pond and giggled with delight at Mrs. Duck and her nearly grown ducklings. Farther back, there was an old barn, hardly more than a foundation and an airy roof joined by rickety walls with many slats missing.

"Here, Miz Jenny!" they would call, surging ahead. "Look, Miz Jenny!"—at a peach tree that still, miraculously, bore peaches, or at a mound of wild marigolds.

Now—looking back with the hideous wisdom of what happened later—I wonder whether they weren't guiding my direction, heading me where they wanted me to go. One or the other was always at my side, and when they called me, I hurried over to wherever they were. I found delight in them, and through them, in my new home. Yet, looking back on it, I see something unnatural in those children, something ominous.

Or is this part of my madness?

No. I am certain of it: they were steering me away from the woods.

The troubled dreams persisted but were formless, and I could not remember them the next day. Several times I awoke at night trembling and afraid to go back to sleep.

My days were crowded. In addition to getting settled, I had to prepare for the imminent opening of school. I saw the children only fleetingly. Some would be walking along the road, or, now and then, they would drop in for a quick visit. Helen came more frequently than the rest, usually with one or two of the others but now and then alone. She never stayed long. In spite of her apparent bravado, there was something shy and reserved about her, and yet, she seemed to be seeking something, to be asking something of me which I could not define. I knew that Helen would be my special little friend—later, when I had the time.

One morning I made a quick trip into town to pick up a book which the library had ordered for me. I had planned to spend the day at home reading. When I returned, there was Brian standing by the back door, staring toward the woods. He jumped when I drove up the driveway, obviously startled.

"Oh—Miz Jenny—you come back!"

"Morning, Brian. How are you?"

"Oh—uh—"

I tried to set him at ease, my mind still mainly on the day's tasks. "Where's everybody? You here by yourself?"

91

"They gone into the woods," he blurted. "I told them not to. But they gone into the woods."

"Oh, Lord." I really didn't have time to fool with any children today. But I didn't want them in those woods. I had visions of snakes and poison ivy and mosquitoes. "Stay here, Brian." I set my books down on the steps and started toward the woods.

"My mother told me not to go in them woods, and I ain't going," Brian was saying behind me. "I told them."

With some trepidation, I went to the fringes of the woods. There was a deer path there. I stood at the path for a moment, thinking of the woods creatures and wondering whether I really wanted to infringe upon their territory. But on some level of myself, I was drawn to the woods, too. There is something compelling about nature unchecked, a little space where man has not yet intruded. Somewhere in there I heard disembodied voices of the children. I went into the woods.

Cool and dark and sheltering. Dusk of dawn. A womb from which there need be no wrenching birth. Scent of pine and wildflowers, spicy and sweet. Birds chirping and the buzz of insects going about their business. The scampering of squirrel feet. A healing place. For an instant I stood there, and the pain and loneliness which I had pushed aside, just in order to cope, rose to my throat, and I knew that if I knelt there in the grass and let the pain come out, I would emerge from the woods healed.

I heard children's laughter closer. Sighing, I went to find them.

They were beyond a copse of young trees. "Oh— Miz Jenny!" Helen, Catherine and Robert, and two others whose names I did not know. They looked strangely guilty, like children caught at mischief.

"Uh—Miz Jenny—we come here to play sometime." Helen, of course.

An old shack. The shell of an old shack. Tottering like an ancient too long out of the grave. Log exterior eaten away by insects and by time. I shivered, suddenly cold.

Helen stepped across the empty doorway. "Come on in, Miz Jenny," she invited like a welcoming hostess. The other children hovered outside around the doorway, silent, waiting.

I entered. The earthen floor was hard, long trampled. Beyond the fresh wood scent was something else—some odor peculiar to this cabin. What? Something old and indefinable. I shivered again.

Along one wall was what remained of a hearth. Along the adjacent wall lay huddled a mass of rotten boards which may have been some piece of furniture but which now was probably the shelter of rats or snakes. What *was* that odor?

"We come here sometimes to play," Helen was saying. "We like it here." Or did she say, "It likes us here?" I was only half-listening.

For I felt a decided Presence in this place. I couldn't—can't—describe it or fasten it down to any particular spot. But I sensed it as clearly as I saw the crumbling hearth and felt the earth beneath my feet. Suddenly, I felt stifled, smothered, a feeling of intolerable claustrophobia. I had to get out of there. Helen chattered on, and the rest of the children had crowded in behind me, blocking the doorway. I had to get out! Had to!

With the last measure of control, I pushed past the children. "Come on. Let's go back to the house." I walked briskly, trying not to yield to panic, out of the woods, back into the sunshine, across the field and to the house, where Brian was sitting on the back steps.

"Brian's a-scared," someone said.

"No such-a thing..."

There was a brief but intense skirmish; then I sent the children home. I stood in my sunny new kitchen and looked out the back window. The scene was rustic, even idyllic, with the lily pond on the left, the sweep of meadow with clumps of wildflowers, and then the woods, lush and inviting.

And in that woody place, hidden by the trees which had grown up around it—that ghost of a cabin, squatting malevolently. Waiting.

---

Some dreams are dreams and some are visions. The first vision came that night.

Long after the children had gone, sitting alone in my study, gazing out the back window at the fringe of woods darkening and then disappearing into night, I kept seeing the old cabin—undoubtedly a slave cabin, built before the trees had grown around it and obscured it. One room where everybody ate, slept, spent whatever leisure there was. I should have been jubilant—here was living history, an artifact to be examined and preserved. Instead I was repelled—no, terrified. What was that impalpable presence that I had sensed? Familiar, awful...?

I turned on the lamp. My books, my desk, already covered with papers, my old typewriter and new computer all restored an aura of reality to my world. I turned from the desk, which faced the window, and sat in my rocking chair putting the finishing touches on the syllabi for my classes.

Later, waiting for sleep to come, I remembered, with a shock, where I had sensed that feeling of an unseen Presence. It was on the night that Edward died. It was on that awful, unthinkable night when I left the hospital alone, after that unending day of the ritual of dying, and then the word, the unbelievable word, and the end of everything, everything! And then, in that empty house filled with sympathetic friends, that alien house where I had lived for so many years, in all of that, calling long-distance to my stranger-sons, I felt this Presence! Edward, my Edward—where?

Tears cooled my face as I slipped into sleep.

*It was like a slow-motion sequence in a black and white movie. All the movements were slow and smooth, as if something had happened to time. The atmosphere was somehow thick. A youngish woman and two little girls in the cabin. A fire in the fireplace, its gray flames licking upward in a slow, lascivious dance. The woman sinking wearily into the rough wooden chair by the fire. The smaller child in her lap. The older girl moving toward the door, slowly, as if walking under water. The mother's head sinking forward, her cheek resting on the little girl's head. The door drifting open and an adolescent boy gliding in, his movements slow and liquid, closing the door after him, starting toward the heavy oak table. His sister following and saying something to him. The door opening again. Everyone turning toward the door. In the doorway a stocky white man.*

Oh, I struggled, I struggled to awaken! I tried to cry out, but nothing came. Finally I came partially to consciousness trembling in the dark, afraid to go back to sleep. I felt that somehow I had slipped out of time, and the very basis of my world had altered. Then sleep came suddenly and completely, like a hood dropped over my head.

Is this where madness began?

# II

The woods, after that night, were sinister. As I gazed at them from the back door or through the window of my study, they seemed to be harboring some obscene secret.

School had opened by now, and I was busy with the reality of lectures to be prepared, new colleagues to get to know, a whole new routine. My classes were in the afternoon, and it was usually around dinnertime before I got home. Sometimes I would surprise two or three children in my yard, heading out. Usually Helen was with them. I wondered whether they had been in the woods; sometimes I admonished them to stay out. But I had the feeling that they had claimed the cabin as theirs, and my warnings were meaningless.

It was Victorine who told me the whispered history of my new home. Victorine was a woman from the nearby housing project, who came once a week to help me clean and to tell me the neighborhood gossip.

"You mean to say, Miz Jenny, ain't nobody told you about this place?" We were pausing for lunch. "Well, I declare."

"No, not really. I figured there was slavery all around here, but other than that, I don't know anything."

She didn't say—but I read it in her face -"and you a history professor!" Professors are supposed to know everything.

"Well—." She put down her fork. Her thin brown face was grave, her graying hair a wispy frame. "It was thisaway, Miz Jenny...."

This house here, this'n wasn't the first. The old house burnt down that night—oh, a tremendous fire, Miz Jenny, destroyed everything, everything. Wasn't many people living out here then, just that slave girl Rachel and her chilrun. Folks said them chilrun was his'n—Tom Murchison's. Folks said it was scandalous the way him and her lived here together after the old folks died, breeding babies. 'Course she was a little bit older than him. Anyways, one night there was this awful fire, and it all burnt down, and when it was all over with and the ashes had done cooled, you know what they found? They found him—or what was left of him—all burnt up in that fire!

"Nobody never seen Rachel and them chilrun after that. Some said they lived wild in the woods—was thick woods all around here then. Oh yes, them white folks looked for them all well 'nough, thinkin' they might've set the fire, which they probably did. But nobody never seen hide nor hair of 'em.

After awhile somebody bought this land from Murchison's sister—she'd done moved north long back, she didn't want no parts of this place—and put up this house. Oh, that was many years later. But seems like nobody was ever satisfied here for very long. Mr. Colson, the man you bought it from, he just used it for a huntin' lodge, brought his friends here for huntin' season and that's all. Never really lived here.

But that ain't the whole story, Miz Jenny. That slave cabin back there, folks say strange things goes on there. That's where Rachel and her chilrun lived. They say that before the trees growed up around it, when you could see it from the road, folks goin' by at night used to see a strange light in the windows, like somebody was in there with a candle. Well, 'course, that's just what people say and you can't put no reliance in that. They do say, though, that Mr. Colson's dogs wouldn't go nowheres near that cabin. My brother, God rest him, he used to work for Mr. Colson on them huntin' parties, and he told me what he seen with his own eyes. Them dogs wouldn't go nowheres near that cabin, don't care what kinda game might be there.

But the worst of it—I don't know whether I ought to tell you this; I don't want to scare you—didn't nobody tell you about the child? Well, my mama used to tell me this story, and folks say it's true. When they went to build this house on the burnt out land, long years after the fire, a workman went to look over the cabin for something or other, not knowin', of course, what folks around here thought about the strange goin's-on there. Well, he went in the door, and there, curled up on the floor by the fireplace, there was a child, long dead! Yes! Rottin' and stinkin'! A child! Oh, I tell you, Miz Jenny, was a time here then! My grandma used to tell me, tryin' to keep us children away from there. A boy, they say. Child didn't have no parents, used to work on a farm for his keep. Slavery was long over then. No more'n twelve or so. No, Miz Jenny, didn't nobody much care then, child didn't have nobody. God knows them white folks he worked for didn't care nothin' about him. But folks around here still stay away from that cabin.

Funny thing, though. Chilrun seem to hang around there don't care what you tell them. I remember when I was little, some of the chilrun I knew used to go there. Mostly, those who didn't have no parents to make them stay away. Funny.

---

Victorine got up to do the dishes and clean out the refrigerator, while I went upstairs to work on the current set of papers. But I was profoundly disturbed by the story. I know that oral history often distorts and exaggerates, but almost always it contains the essence of the truth. Long after Victorine had gone, I kept hearing her voice, intense and compelling, kept seeing her glittering eyes and gesturing hands as she recounted the multiple tragedies of this place which I now owned. Beyond her words, she seemed somehow ancient and yet timeless. Even the reality of the papers I was grading, with their grammatical peculiarities and creative spelling, could not pull me away from Victorine's tale. What it omitted was just as scary as what it revealed. What was the whole story? Who was Rachel, and what had been her life?

That night I had to go back to school to a faculty meeting. For an hour or so the story's spell faded, drowned in the petty concerns which typify faculty meetings. But as I drove up the dark road home, I thought again about Rachel and her children, about Murchison's fiery end, about the peculiar fact of the unknown child who had curled up before the cold hearth and died.

The night was pitch black, with stars and moon obscured by clouds. Only my headlights cut into the darkness: ahead, behind, and on either side there was only dark. Again, I had the feeling of being lost in time. An occasional house light, a mailbox along the road, a recognizable tree here and there reassured me that I was on the right way. It was a relief to bear left at the old church crossroad and know that home was just up the hill. Around the now familiar curves, past the three weeping willows, and then slowing in front of my house.

O God! O God! I was gripped by terror! For there, on my door—the carved sun was glowing, glowing—in the dark of that black night, that sun was glowing! A ghastly, malevolent glow, bright as a neon light. Disembodied in the surrounding dark.

I panicked. With a screech of tires, I jolted up the hill, speeding wildly into the blackness of the night, turning this way and that on the winding roads, past pastures and barns and farm houses. I was soon lost, but then where could I go? I was a ship plowing an unknown ocean, rushing madly nowhere.

Finally I stopped, exhausted, and leaning my head on the steering wheel, I wept. After awhile I quieted and simply sat there, not knowing what to do. Staring into the darkness, I could see nothing but shadow shapes. Closing my eyes I saw again that weird glow on my door, like a sick sun menacing the world.

I flicked my eyes open and sat there, gripping the steering wheel, staring into darkness with the unblinking, unseeing gaze of the dead. I was terrified of the images that lay behind my eyes. Desperately, I battled the sheer physical exhaustion which made my head nod and my lids slip shut.

Without wishing to, I dozed.

I jerked awake, chilled and nervous. Now there were streaks of ruddy light in the sky, and it was dawn. My mouth was fuzzy; my back ached. I had been in the same clothes since yesterday, and my need for the bathroom was urgent. Wearily, I started the car. I drove until I found a main road, then headed home.

In the gray morning, the house was as ordinary as ever. I began to doubt that I had really seen anything unusual. A reflection from my headlights perhaps? Or perhaps nothing at all—this may have been an illusion springing from Victorine's story. Why had it frightened me so?

Perhaps—for the first time I really began to wonder—perhaps I was losing my mind.

Certainly I was obsessed. Victorine's story was like a light clicking on inside myself. I needed to know what had happened in that slave cabin, what had happened in the house which had been consumed by fire. I began using the skills of my profession. I began searching old newspapers and histories in the nearby libraries. I wrote to the Recorder of Deeds. I tracked down records of births and marriages, taxes and deaths. Back in Washington for the Christmas break, I spent my days searching through archives, seeking census reports, poring through materials at the Library of Congress. My friends thought I was doing research for a scholarly paper. I was doing research for my life!

I returned home with notes to assemble and materials to study. Many nights, stopping to take off my glasses and rest my eyes, I wondered whether the sun on my front door was glowing. I shivered and shoved the thought aside.

When it was all done, all gathered and assembled, it still wasn't enough. I needed more.

*oh babe, oh babe...it's so good...oh babe so good so good...and my whole self was aflame with passion, and he thrust deep, deep into the core of my self, and my legs were clasped around his back pushing him deeper and oh babe oh babe it's so good, and our hands clasped above my head. and faster and faster so good and he cried out and....*

I awoke in ecstatic spasm and in tears. I awoke crying at the cruelty of the dream, to arouse in me old passion, past ecstasy which could never be repeated. Edward! After all these many months, Edward!

But no, I was not awake! For I could still hear the sounds of passion, where?—here in this room? In the hall? The study? Where?—woman sobs; inarticulate groans and grunts, deep-voiced, rising to a crescendo, the cry, and then the sigh, and then something muttered. And still the sobbing....

And fury burst through my horror and I sat upright in bed and screamed, "Damn you! Damn you! Dead things...." Then fear flooded me, and I cowered beneath the covers like a frightened child and lay there trembling until, unbidden and unwanted, sleep came.

---

"Miz Jenny—" Victorine seemed uneasy. She had not been her usual amiable self this morning, and now she had turned off the vacuum cleaner and come over to where I was going through the motions of looking for my gloves. Miz Jenny—somebody asked me to tell you something."

I sighed impatiently. The dream of Rachel and her lover still held me in its grip. I was nervous and irritable. "What did I do with those gloves? Did you see them upstairs anywhere?"

"No ma'am." She didn't usually call me "ma'am." We had gotten past that early on. She had sensed my irritability. The "ma'am" had an edge to it.

"Oh, Victorine, I didn't mean to snap at you." I gave up the search for the gloves and flopped onto the sofa. "You were about to tell me something."

"A old lady at the home where my aunt stays—she wants to see you."

"See me? I don't know any old lady at any home. You sure she wants me?"

Victorine was fiddling around dusting. But her face was troubled. "Well, Miz Jenny, we all know—us that's been here all this time we know how you live in this house and fixing it up and all, and this old lady, Miss Dorrie Jenson, she heard about it, too."

"I didn't know I was the subject of so much interest." But Victorine ignored my sarcasm, and I was sorry I had said that.

"I go see about my aunt whenever I can, and last time I was there—Sunday it was—Miss Dorrie asked me to tell you. "

"What does she want with me?"

"Says she got something to tell you. But Miz Jenny, you don't have to feel like you really gotta go there. Miss Dorrie is awful old, and she gets notions. Her mind comes and goes. But she asked me awful strong to tell you, so I did."

"Something to tell me about what? About this house? Does she know something?"

"I don't know, probably so." Victorine had stopped dusting by now and was sitting on the edge of the radiator, fingering the dust cloth absently. "She always was a kinda peculiar person. Never got married, lived all by herself in that little house. Now her mind is bad, and she says some outlandish things. I wouldn't bother if I was you, Miz Jenny."

But I did bother. After a peaceful night's sleep, my obsession returned, and I took my tape recorder and went to find Miss Dorrie Jenson. I was convinced by now that the house's awful secrets were not to be found in the documents I had so carefully searched.

The Baptist Home for the Aged (the Black aged) was an almost surrealistic world. You stepped out of the lemon-sunshine of a January morning and into a shadowed world of half-death. The smell of stale urine hovered like a poisonous vapor, and here and there along the bare walls crouched an old person, a bundle of rags through which ancient eyes silently watched.

At the receptionist's direction I passed through the corridor to a large day room. I paused at the door, momentarily overwhelmed. There was over all a stench of decay. Masses of flesh in wheelchairs, twisted bodies on crutches, bony forms huddled under gray sheets on cots, some sprawled on rickety chairs, some sitting on the floor, all silent, waiting, waiting, while a television set in the middle of the room blared out its cheery message of the benefits of Nouvelle Beauty Soap.

With the help of a gaunt sallow-faced nurse, I found Miss Dorrie Jenson nodding in a lounge chair in a corner. She seemed in better shape than most. Her eyes brightened when I introduced myself, and when she took me to her room across the hall, she walked fairly briskly, though she leaned heavily on a cane. She was spare, despite her years—which must have been considerable, judging from her fallen, copiously wrinkled face and scant white hair.

Later I played the tape over and over again. I wasn't sure how much was truth and how much was the delusion of senility. I just didn't know. And when Victorine came again and told me that Miss Dorrie was down real sick, and then when she called me a few days later and told me that Miss Dorrie was dead, I played the tape again and yet again. I saw the glitter of her yellowed eyes, I felt her hot foul breath through the snaggled teeth, I felt the grip of her skinny hand on my wrist.

And as I listened, as I listened again, I knew, yes I knew that Miss Dorrie spoke truth.

------

Well now, Missus [after some preliminary awkwardness the tape gets underway here], you heared some things about the house where you livin', but the half ain't yet been told. I know some things that don't nobody else know, and I reckon it's time I passed them on—before [dry chuckle here] I passes on myself. Some things ought not to die just 'cause the people that lived 'em is gone. I never told nobody, first 'cause I was 'fraid, then 'cause there wasn't nobody I wanted to tell, then 'cause there just wasn't no point in tellin'. But you's there now, and I

hear tell you means to stay. Ain't no colored ever had
that house 'cepting you. So I wanted you to know,
and I'm glad you finally come to see me.

[Long pause here. I thought Miss Dorrie had
drifted off to sleep. Maybe she had.]

Musta been near 'bout fifty year ago—more, I
reckon—back in the Depression days—I used to
work in that house. It was just for a little while, and
folks here has forgot, them what ever knowed. Some
white folks named Ogden lived here then. It wasn't
but the three of them—him and her and the child.
The child. A little girl, Missus, around three-four
year old. Stella.

Sickly child. Always seemed to catch cold, even
in the summer time. Real pale-like but with a head
full of curly dark hair like her mama's. Mr. Ogden he
was tall and full-muscled with blond hair; even his
eyelashes was blond. But he wasn't pale like that
child. Seem like his wife was some kinda foreigner,
brownish with all that dark hair. I don't know. They
come in the springtime. Hadn't nobody lived there
for a long time. They got me in to do the housework
and tend the child.

Well, Missus, wasn't long before I seen that there
was something wrong with that child. Wouldn't talk.
All them months I was there, I never heard her say a
word. Nary a word. She could make noises if she got
real riled or wanted something real bad, but nary a
word would she say. Her ma and pa, they sorta left
her to me. They was peculiar people, seemed like
each one was livin' there alone. But the child she
clung to me like I was her mama. Nights, I slept in a
cot in her room. Sometimes she would have a scary
dream and come creepin' into my bed and lay there
shiverin' like a scared puppy, and I would hold her
until we both went back to sleep. Days, she would
play outside in the yard. Seem like she was more
easy in herself when she was outside the house. And

seem like she would always end up in that
cabin—that slave cabin where that woman Rachel
used to live with her chilrun. Whenever I missed her
and couldn't find her, there she'd be, somewhere
around that cabin. Stella.

It wasn't a easy time of life for me. I wasn't
young even then, and I was at that age when women
begins to see their life passin' them by, and they ain't
had nothin' much but work, work, work, and look
like that's all there's ever gonna be. Times was awful
hard, and white folks was meaner than ever. We was
scared, yes colored folks was scared and mad, too.
Well.

[Another long pause]

This ain't easy to tell. Come fall, the child was
down sick real bad. Terrible cough, hot-hot to touch,
eyes way too bright. Weak, real weak. Just laid
there, not hardly moving. Missus, I tried not to love
that child. Colored folks ain't got no business lovin'
white folks, even chilrun, 'cause white folks is done
us so terrible. But you can't take care of nothin', not
even a sick kitten, without sooner or later you comes
to love her.

But it ain't that simple.

That night, it was one of them warm, full moon
nights, all the sweeter 'cause you knows winter is
coming. Stella was real sick, like I said. Her folks
had long gone to bed. And she was quiet. Missus, I
really thought she was better, I really did. She was
sleepin' mighty sound.

Well, I left the house. No, I ain't gon talk about
that. But I was a woman even so, and I wasn't young
no more, but I still felt what women is meant to feel,
and it was one of them full moon nights, and the
grass was sweet down by the pond. And he was—but
no, I ain't gon talk about that.

It was just startin' to get light when I come
tippin' back into that house, into that room. I was
kinda nervous, 'cause I'd stayed longer than I'd
intended. But the room was quiet, and I said to
myself that everything was all right and that Stella
had slept through the night and maybe she would
get well now. So I went over to her bed, and all of a
sudden I knew—the room was too quiet. Wasn't
nobody there but me!

I turned on the lamp, and Missus, it was true!
Stella was gone! Missus, I was a crazy woman, right
then and there! First I thought that she might be in
her folks' room, but somehow I knew she wasn't. I
went flyin' all over that house, then outside in the
yard, callin', callin', but gettin' no answer. "Stella!
Stella!" Knowin' she wouldn't, couldn't answer,
'cause she couldn't talk. And then I knew! I ran—O
Lord, I ran—to the cabin. I recollect how strange it
was, in that early light just at day-clean, with the
trees lookin' tall, tall and every blade of grass
standin' up by itself, and how it smelled of fresh day
and my own fear.

Well, I bust in the doorway, and there on the dirt
floor in front of the fireplace, there she was. My little
Stella, little sick baby, not sick no more. Not never
sick no more.

[Pause]

Missus, I can't tell you what I felt right then. I
just can't tell you. But one thing riz up above
everything. I couldn't let nobody know what
happened. Missus, I hadn't never handled no dead
body before, and I dreaded to touch her. But I'd done
left this white child when I was supposin' to be takin'
care of her, and she'd come out there, God knows
how, and now she was dead. In them days niggers
was lynched for less than that. So I went over to that
poor little body, and I picked her up and her head
fell back over my arm, and her legs flopped as I ran.

And I prayed to God it wasn't light enough for
nobody to see me and I tiptoed up them steps hopin'
that if them Ogdens come out of their room, I would
just go on and finish dyin', thinkin' that my breath
was so loud it would rouse them, feelin' them little
legs flop-floppin' against me.

I stuffed her into her bed, just like she'd been
there all night, and covered her up. I put on my
night clothes and mussed up my hair. And, Missus, I
said a prayer for her and for me. Then I went bangin'
on their door cryin' out for them to come, come see
about their child.

Oh, Missus there's something odd about that
cabin! Something draws chilrun to it. My little
Stella, she wasn't the first nor yet the last. I done
lived a long time now, and there's things I knows.
Once in a great while somethin' happens—somethin'
so dreadful that it leaves traces of itself long, long
after the people is dust. Somethin' happened there,
Missus. Can't you feel it? Take heed, Missus. Take
heed.

---

I turned off the tape and sat thinking for a long
time. After a while, I wandered over to the window
and stood gazing at the woods, calm and inviting in
the winter dusk. I stood for a long time, letting Miss
Dorrie's tale sink in, hearing her words in the
silence of approaching night. I came back to the
present with a jolt: a small shadow slipped out of the
woods and went running across my back yard. I
raised the window and shouted, "Helen! Helen, is
that you? You better go home!" And now, in the
floodlight over my back step, I could see her. She
waved and ran in the direction of home. And I felt a
special, unaccountable fear.

*Obscene whispers and the bed squeaking faster
and faster the smell of raw sex and he oh Rachel
Rachel and she saying nothing this time nothing and*

*faster and faster and he only grunting now and
faster and then the cry the cry a scream now a death
scream and she shrieking my chilrun my chilrun
where my chilrun and he bitch you black bitch and
she grunting as the knife went in again and the smell
of sex the smell of blood the smell of death and now
the flames licking upward licking crackling fire
searing burning and the stench of smoke and blood
and burning flesh and Rachel's screams and fire
consuming all purifying all cleansing fire, purifying
all and I awoke with the stench of love and death in
my nostrils and whirling in my head the roar of fire
and Rachel's crazy laughter....*

# III

It was mid-winter by now, and the days were
gloomy. Instead of fluffy white snow to be greeted
with joy, we had, on the worst days, sleet and slush.
Some mornings I would find that snow had fallen
during the night. Looking out of my study window, I
saw how serene was the expanse between house and
woods, the thin layer of white covering everything,
the bare trees austere and lovely, their shadows
making patterns in the snow. Soon the fragile white
would vanish in the sun. But for a few moments, in
all that beauty, my spirit would be at peace.

The dream was gentle, easing me out of sleep.
Edward was already up, rattling round the kitchen,
fixing breakfast. The inviting aromas of morning
melted the vestiges of sleep—coffee and bacon, even
rolls rising in the oven. I stretched lazily and pulled
the covers up to my chin. In a minute he would be
here, in that raggedy old robe of his, grinning and
carrying a tray....

I sat straight up in bed, my eyes staring. O my
God! Edward was dead! and I was here, here in this
haunted place. And who—what—was in my kitchen?

For I could still hear the clink of silverware on dishes, still smell food cooking! And now there were voices, muffled and indistinct. And now a child's laugh!

I crept out of bed, trembling. Could Victorine have come in early—or was this even her day? I stumbled to the front window, but no car was outside except mine, covered with the dusting of snow which had fallen overnight. The child's laugh again—and a hushed admonition from someone. Bacon and rolls cooking. There was something eery about this unaccountable Presence. My scalp tingled, and I could not contain the rising panic.

Oh, I must run—get out—where? Irrationally, I grabbed my car keys from my purse. How to get out? Not by downstairs! I darted about the room, from door to window, like something trapped. I ran to the den and peered out the back window. And O God! O God! Footprints! Footprints in the snow! *Footprints*—from the ring of woods to my back door. From the cabin! Several sets, one set veering away from the others and back, like a child scampering in capricious joy.

"Rachel!" I whispered.

And the laughter of the child became the crazed laughter of a madwoman, and the aroma of food became the stench of burning flesh. And I fled in panic to my bed and, like a child, pulled the covers over my head and cowered there, under the flimsy protection of a sheet and comforter, praying for deliverance.

Perhaps I slept. When I finally sat on the edge of the bed and thrust my cold feet into my slippers, the sun was high. The house was silent. I crept to the window and looked out. By now the sun had melted the snow except for patches of white in shaded spots. Had there really been footprints? Had it all been a dream? Or was I losing my mind?

Not a dream. For my purse lay open on the floor.
And still clutched in my hand, hot and damp, were
my car keys.

---

These were frightful times. I feared sleep
because of the dreams, visions. Evenings when I
came home after dark, I was afraid to look at my
front door, lest the carved sun be glowing, glowing
again. I was afraid to go into the woods, because I
was convinced by now that the cabin was haunted.
That *I* was haunted—or mad. Probably that. I didn't
believe in ghosts, but I did believe in madness.

My colleagues, not having known me before, did
not suspect that I was different from what I had ever
been. And I had made no friends. None but
Victorine, who kept a worried eye on me.

And Helen. My little friend, who came more and
more often to keep me company, first on weekend
afternoons and then on winter evenings, when I had
to drive her home. Her mother worked, and her
Uncle Jason was there in the afternoons when Helen
came home from school. Jason did odd jobs and
looked for work, but mostly he was home.

Helen, I found, was a strange little girl. She
hungered in a way which I understood. She
hungered for everything. She ate ravenously
whatever I put before her, but her hunger was
deeper than that. She was curious about everything,
read my books (even the ones she couldn't possibly
understand), asked questions until, in my own
disturbed state, I was driven to distraction,
chattered on endlessly about everything in the
world. She was a toucher. She hugged me when she
came and hugged me when she left. She touched my
shoulder when she passed my chair, squeezed my
hand, even wanted to comb my hair. Then she would
be quiet for hours reading or doing her homework.

She was with me in many dark hours, and with her vibrant presence, she chased the ghosts away—so to speak.

But she, too, had her dark side.

"What's wrong with your face?" I asked one Saturday afternoon. We had just gotten into the car, headed for town to the supermarket. In the afternoon light I saw that her jaw was swollen.

"Nothing, Miz Jenny. Nothing wrong with my face." She turned away.

"No, here." I turned her toward me and gently ran my fingers over the swelling. "What is this? Do you have a bad tooth?"

"Yes'm. A bad tooth." It was as if a curtain had descended. She was silent as we drove down the hill and did not resume her usual chatter until we pulled into the supermarket parking lot.

Her eyes held a sadness which I could not fathom.

By now my obsession with the secret of the house had intensified. It whispered behind every word, lingered beneath every thought. I wonder now why I didn't just leave, right in the middle of the semester, and go back to Washington. But I had already burned my bridges. There was no "back" to go to. And besides, something in me was too stubborn to give up before the end. So I stayed.

Teachers have a secret source of wisdom: if you want to know anything, ask the students. I made the assignment to my seniors knowing full well what I was seeking. They were to interview elderly people about past events. Then we would compile an oral history of the area and verify what we could through various kinds of official records. It was a good research project in oral history. But in the depths of my being, I was hoping that some student would

pull out from some ancient memory the clue I was
seeking.

The results of the assignment were not
promising, at least not for my purposes. The papers
came in on a Friday, and I spent that evening poring
through, searching in vain for any mention of Rachel
or the old Murchison place. Nothing. The teacher in
me took over and appreciated the zeal with which
the youngsters had talked with grandparents and
great-aunts and frail old neighbors. One—Cynthia
Eddings, of course—had even gone to the home
where Miss Dorrie had lived, and interviewed
residents there. (And I thought of Miss Dorrie. I
heard again her wispy old voice passing on to me her
dread secret.) But there was no mention of the
Murchison place.

Saturday passed in a fog of depression. I went
over the papers again, jotting notes and making
suggestions for further research. The neighborhood
children came on Saturday afternoon, as usual, to
play in my back yard and to wander into the woods.
Helen stayed behind, and we shared a supper of
chicken wings and beans and salad. She was
unusually chatty that evening, and after awhile her
rapid staccato of talk began to get on my nerves.

"Helen," I said finally, "it's dark out now. I'd
better drive you home. Your mother will be worried."

"Mama said it was all right for me to stay
awhile. She knows I'm here. You want me to call her
back? She won't care if I stay."

We had cleared up the dishes by now and were
closing the drapes in the living room, preparing for
night.

"Well, tell you what. We'll look at TV for awhile,
and then I'll run you home." We would both be
soothed by television's hypnotic spell.

The doorbell jerked us out of some Disney fantasy. Peering through the window in the front door, I didn't know the man who stood on my porch, taking a long drag from a cigarette. The cigarette glowed, a spot of fire in the night, then dimmed in a yellow arc as he lowered it from his lips.

"Who is it?" I called.

"I come for Helen. Her uncle Jason."

I hesitated to open the door. There was something sinister in his posture. Helen was right beside me. "It's your uncle," I said.

"Jason." For the first time today her voice was low.

I opened the door. The man was young, hardly older than my students. He was a smooth tan, what we used to call "tantalizin' brown."

"How d'you do, Dr. Watts. Jason Taylor here. Helen's uncle."

"Come right in. She's ready to go. I'm sorry I kept her so long. We were watching TV...."

Helen made no move to get her coat.

"Where Mama?"

"In the car." He gestured vaguely toward the closed door. I glanced out the window, and there was indeed a car out there, its motor running, its headlights piercing the dark.

"Hurry up, Helen," I said. "Your mother's waiting." She turned silently and went to get her things.

Jason stood comfortably in the hallway, his hands in his jacket pockets. His quick glance around seemed to take in everything. I said, too loudly, "She'll be right back. Would you like to sit down?" He looked me full in the face, smiled, and shook his head. His eyes were long-lashed and, surprisingly, light brown. In that instant, in a flash of feeling, I

114

was acutely aware of my graying hair and of the lines which were beginning to define my face, and I wished myself young again. And I hated him for that. The feeling flashed and faded in an instant, but it left damage in its wake. *Where* was Helen?

She came, dawdling, not anxious to leave. She was bundled up; still, I was vaguely worried that her thin coat and small hat were insufficient to keep out the cold.

"Goodnight, Miz Jenny," she muttered.

"Goodnight, Helen. See you soon."

At the window I watched them down the walk. He put his arm around her, drawing her closer against the cold. He said something to her, but her head was down, her form huddled into itself in the wind. At the car he opened the front door and the lights came on briefly while she got in, then again when he slid into the driver's seat. I turned from the window, grateful for the quiet, soothed by the somnolent murmuring of the TV.

But deep down inside was a growing feeling of apprehension. Wrapped in my own thoughts, I had missed—something. I went into the den to turn off the TV. I would spend the rest of the evening recording the grades for the oral history project and searching the papers again for some clue, anything, to my own dilemma.

And there, on my rocker in front of the television set, were Helen's gloves. I was annoyed. Children were so careless! It was cold and she would need those gloves. Well, maybe she would come and get them, or I would call her house in the morning or drop them off sometime tomorrow. But as I gathered the papers and my record book, I kept seeing those forlorn little gloves dropped so carelessly in my chair.

Something was not right. What had I missed?

Then suddenly I knew—Helen's mother—She was not in the car!

----

Sunday was bright and cheery, warm for winter. I went to church and came back refreshed. Restored, perhaps. I called my sons as I often did on a Sunday afternoon, and we had the usual harried long distance conversation of how-ya-doing-fine-what's happening, the usual hi-Grandma from the children, the usual polite nothings from long distance daughters-in-law. I wondered how they really were and wished that there were one in the lot to whom I could tell my trouble. But when Kenneth in Cleveland said, "It's snowing like hell here, how's everything in the sunny South?" I said, "Fine," and talked about the weather. And when David in Los Angeles asked, "You still okay there by yourself, Mom?" I wanted to tell him the truth, but I heard little voices in the background yelling, "Lemme talk to Grandma....No, me first...." and I just said, "Sure."

Later, that evening as I was dozing away *60 Minutes*, the doorbell rang.

"Who is it?"

"It's me, Dr. Watts—Kelvin Adams."

Then I remembered. Kelvin was the only student (except Jay McDowell, of course) who had not turned in his oral history project. Good heavens, he could turn it in on Monday. Why was he at my door on Sunday evening? Did he expect me to spend my Sunday evening reading his paper?

"Dr. Watts, I'm sorry to bother you at home, but I really wanted to tell you about this." Somehow, even in his senior year, Kelvin had not outgrown an adolescent awkwardness, and his big, athletic body seemed a perpetual source of surprise to him, as if it had happened while his attention was diverted. Kelvin was in college on a football scholarship, but he was a budding writer. Kelvin reminded me of my own sons in their younger years, in the waning years of our closeness, before they had finished growing up and growing away.

"Come on in, Kelvin. Sit down a minute."

"Dr. Watts, this just couldn't wait 'til tomorrow. I just got back, and I wanted to tell you right away."

We settled on the sofa.

"Dr. Watts, I'm sorry my project is late. I haven't had a chance to write it up. But I wanted you to hear this—'cause it's about your place."

"Kelvin—you found out something? Who'd you interview? What—?"

He grinned, and I think he enjoyed my sudden fluster. I saw myself sitting there in my loafing clothes—sloppy pants, flannel shirt, and no girdle and realized that Kelvin had ferreted out a different me from the staid Dr. Watts.

"I went over to Garrison Crossroads to see my grandma. I couldn't go before because she's been kinda sick. She's really old, Dr. Watts, and she doesn't always feel like talking. You know where Garrison Crossroads is? Over toward the mountain, about fifty miles from here." His eyes sparkled, and his words tumbled all over each other. "Anyway, she's been living there since I was little, when she went to live with my Aunt Lettie. But she used to live here, so I thought I'd interview her for my project." He smiled apologetically. "I tried some other people, Dr. Watts, but nobody told me much. So I waited 'til Aunt Lettie said it was all right, and then my mom and me went on up to Garrison to talk with Grandma. I don't have a tape recorder, but I took some notes."

He was driving me wild with all these preliminaries. "Kelvin, what did she tell you?"

I believe that he was enjoying my suspense. "Dr. Watts, she told me that 'way long time ago her grandma was a slave not far from the Murchison place, about down where the projects are now. And her grandma told her something about that slave woman who used to live here—that Rachel."

My heart began to thump. "Tell me!"

Kelvin's grandmother had heard this from her mother. Young Sally (later Kelvin's great-great-grandmother) used to go to the Murchisons' occasionally on errands and to play with Rachel's children. Sally was about the age of Rachel's older daughter. She remembered Rachel as a handsome woman, full brown, with long heavy hair which she wore in a braid rather than wrapped in a headkerchief like most of the slave women.

One day Sally went there to bring some eggs (amazing, the details old people remember), and Rachel wasn't there. Tom Murchison himself took the eggs and paid her and told her to hurry on home. She saw the children, all three, standing together looking sort of "odd," as she remembered, their eyes all big, the older girl holding the little one's hand and the brother standing near but not touching. She said howdy to them, but they just stood there looking awful strange.

A few days later, on a Sunday, when the slaves had leisure, she came back to play. As she opened the gate Rachel came running toward her, crazy, her long hair unraveled, her face desperate. "Where my chilrun, Sally? You seen them? They at your place? Where my chilrun?"

"My granny says that's what her mom told her. She was scared of Rachel—she never saw her nor anybody act like that. She ran on home. But the next night or two, that place burnt down, and she figured that she was the last one outside of that house to see Rachel. My granny told me."

I gazed absently at Kelvin for a long time. After awhile he started fidgeting, and then he said, "Dr. Watts, what do you know about this place? There've been all kinds of weird stories—I guess you've heard them. Nobody's ever lived here long, not since the old house burnt down. Have you found out anything about what really happened here?"

"Kelvin, I think—" I stopped. How could I tell a student that I thought my house was haunted? "I think that I'd better make us some coffee."

Sipping coffee in the kitchen, we talked long into the night. Kelvin was the sounding board I needed to bring everything into some kind of perspective. I told him about my research into the property's past—but not Miss Dorric's secret.

"The original house was built in the early eighteen-somethings, apparently by two brothers named Daniel and Theodore Murchison and their parents," I told him. "I couldn't find out who they were or where they came from. The farm must have done pretty well, because they kept buying more land and more slaves to work it."

Kelvin put some more milk in his coffee. "Census reports?"

"And land transfers and whatever. After awhile Dan got married, and the brother disappeared from the records—probably moved away. This Rachel appears in the census of 1830; she was nine then, the child of one of the slaves. Tom, Dan's son, was four. He had two older sisters. I don't know what happened to the mother. I couldn't find any burial record, but she wasn't in that census." I stirred my coffee absently. "Well, the old place started not doing so well. The old folks died; one sister died. The slaves disappeared from census reports. Died, sold, run away—who knows what happens to slaves?"

Kelvin sighed, then smiled the way you do when something hurts, and there's not a thing you can do about it. "This place really has some history in it, doesn't it? Every single one of those slaves had a story."

"Yes, every one. But we'll never know." I wondered to myself how much of the southern landscape is haunted by restless ghosts of slaves. "Anyway, the farm must not have prospered so well after awhile. Tom Murchison kept selling the land piece by piece until next to nothing was left. By the census of 1850 the other sister had left (my friend Victorine tells me that she moved north), and there was nobody else on the farm but the slave Rachel and her two children, a boy five and a girl three."

"That's weird," said Kelvin. "Just him and Rachel and her children?"

"Apparently they were his children, too," I said. "I wonder about that—how she felt about him." I heard again the strange duet of his passion and her sobs, and I shuddered. To be used like a farm implement—I couldn't bear to think of that, right here, right on this soil. "Do you think she might have cared for him?"

"Do *you* think so—really?"

"After all, they'd been raised together, maybe they cared about each other some kind of way."

"Miz Jenny, [in the spell of our conversation he had slipped unconsciously into the name that they all probably called me behind my back], Tom was the master, and Rachel was the slave. He had all the power and she had none. How do you think they could care about each other?"

I shuddered again. Kelvin's common sense had snatched away the flimsy veil with which I had protected myself from the full realization of Rachel's degradation, the full horror of her day-to-day life. But I couldn't talk about that to Kelvin. I got up to refill our mugs.

We talked about what their world must have been like: civil war looming ever closer, another child born, Tom struggling to keep things going, maybe hiring people to do what slaves had done long ago, Rachel being house slave, mother, field hand, unwilling concubine, prisoner to Tom's whims.

"But things must have turned around for him somewhere along the line," I said, remembering suddenly a little piece of information I had found. "Just before he died, he bought back a good piece of the land."

"And then—what? The fire? What happened? Folks say that Rachel set that fire, and then she and the children ran away. Do you think she did? What happened?"

Here my whole system broke down. I couldn't tell Kelvin the terrible things I had seen in nightmares. What had propelled them to the fatal night of passion and murder?

Kelvin left shortly, elated that he had learned so much about my mysterious house. At the door, he turned and asked earnestly, "Miz Jenny, that cabin in the back—she lived there, didn't she? Do kids still go in there to play? I never used to, when I was a kid." He laughed nervously. "It always seemed kinda spooky."

I felt odd as I went upstairs to the den. We had talked too long about this thing. I couldn't shake a strange discomfort. Late as it was, I sat in my rocking chair thinking, rocking, picturing the people whose lives—and deaths—were now so real. My eyes closed as I rocked and thought and felt.

And the air grew thick again. I turned my head, and through my closed lids, I saw her there in the doorway. She was surrounded by a sparkling white light, a living light sparkling like Fourth of July flares. Her hair whipped wildly about her head, her dress billowed as if buffeted by winds. I struggled now to open my eyes, and she was still there. Paralyzed, I clutched the arm of the rocker, my heart pounding so hard that I knew that I would die. My breath came in tortured jerks. Rachel extended one hand, the fingers reaching out for me; the other hand clutched her throat. I opened my mouth to scream, but nothing would come. She began to walk toward me.

And then the world went black.

# IV

When I came back to myself, still sitting in the rocker, night had faded into a new morning. And now I knew that unless I discovered the secret of the house and unless something could be done to rectify history, neither Rachel nor I would have peace. She was trying to frighten me away. But something deep inside told me that if I left, some new horror would happen.

*"Where my chilrun?"* That dreadful cry reverberated in the core of my being. Pausing at my work to rest my eyes or just sitting alone in the house, I could see Rachel, tall and striking, her heavy hair tumbled, her face agonized, crying out for her lost children. I did see her in dreams—long, involved dreams, which I remembered now only in fragments. But even as I awoke, the room was filled with her sobs.

Once I went down to the cabin alone, thinking that by facing my phantoms I would exorcise them. Again the woods were welcoming. But the cabin crouched there ominously, a marvel of decay. I wondered what had held it together for more than a century. I stood in the empty doorway and gazed at the ruined hearth where two children had come to die. And I felt again that Presence, palpable and terrifying. I was standing in the midst of my own nightmares. I muffled a scream. I backed away from the cabin, then turned and ran, feeling a hundred demons at my back.

I was profoundly depressed. With all that terror bottled up inside me, alone in my desperation, I felt cut off from the rest of the world. I felt separated from everyone who glanced at me and didn't see me, didn't know my agony. I felt adrift in time. Only Victorine noticed how haggard and how nervous I had become. And I did feel better on the days when she came. The purr of the vacuum in another room, Victorine's soft humming as she worked, the sight of Victorine herself, spare and strong, a cloth tied around her hair—these things brought an air of normality to this cursed place. She extended her day now, beyond the agreed-upon quitting time until she had to go home to see about the grandchildren who came after school. I could have talked to Victorine. But I didn't want to talk about Rachel any more. I was afraid of what the talk would elicit. Something in me was frozen. I felt myself withdrawing more and more. Even Helen's visits did little now to assuage my gloom.

I was convinced that I was going mad. In a desperate attempt to maintain what hold I had on sanity, I tried to become more involved in professional activities. Late in February, I went to Washington for a conference on nineteenth century slavery. I stayed an extra day or two to look up some documents at the Library of Congress for a project I had long since abandoned but now was thinking of starting again. And there I came across the last link in the story of Rachel—the vital link which would finally set me free.

I was searching microfilms of old newspapers for advertisements for runaway slaves. I really, for the moment, had thrust aside the Rachel mystery; weeks ago I had searched the one local newspaper of her time, but so many issues were missing, I had found nothing. Now I was relieved to have a respite from the pressure of my mad thoughts and looked eagerly for information for my project.

Somehow I happened upon a newspaper from a little town thirty miles or so from my house, a considerable distance in Rachel's time. It didn't nonentity like Tom Murchison would travel that far. So I had only my work on my mind as I perused the issue of October 8, 1857. But century-old newspapers have a fascination of their own, and as usual, I found myself glancing through the articles. And there it was: *MISS JEFFERSON'S FIANCE DEAD IN FIRE*

> The *Courier* was shocked to learn of the untimely demise of Mr. Thomas Murchison of Grace County, in a fire that destroyed his home.

> Mr. Murchison was the beloved of our own Miss Joyce Jefferson, daughter of Mr. and Mrs. Alvin R. Jefferson of Hilltop Mansion. The couple was to be wed at Christmas time. Condolences to Miss Joyce.

Oh! A chill ran up the back of my legs, up my spine, and into my scalp. That was it! And suddenly, there in the silence of the Library of Congress, I knew that this was the piece of information I'd been seeking.

"Oh my God!" I muttered to myself "Tom Murchison got himself engaged to this girl, daughter prominent family in another town. Oh Lord! He was going to bring her there to be mistress over Rachel and her children—their children. That white woman would've made their life hell." But my mind was still groping. Was that enough to warrant the viciousness of the murder? "Hilltop Mansion" sounded pretty fabulous. How was he going to bring her to his poor home, with all the land gone? But no, he had just bought back some of the land, just before—

How'd he raise that money? The question, for some reason, troubled me. How had he, dirt poor, raised that money? Suddenly, I remembered what the little slave girl Sally had seen—Rachel gone and the children standing together looking "odd"—And then I knew—I knew—*He had sold the children!*

My cry of "No!" shattered the quiet. I jumped up, leaving the microfilm in the machine, grabbed my coat and purse, and fled.

He had sold the children! Sent Rachel away on some pretext—and when she returned, her children were gone! Sold! *Where my chilrun?*

On the subway back to the hotel, my mind worked feverishly. Rachel—desperately seeking throughout time, seeking beyond death, seeking her lost children! Now I groaned, and the woman in front of me turned and asked anxiously, "You okay, honey?" And I nodded. But I was not okay.

For now I remembered the children drawn to the cabin, children who, Victorine said, didn't have anybody to warn them away. Didn't have anybody! And two who had come there to die, a nameless boy of twelve or so—the same age as Rachel's son—and a little girl three or four—the age of Rachel's baby. Unloved children, unwanted children. And now Rachel was looking for a girl of ten or eleven. O my God! Helen!

At the hotel, I called Helen's house frantically, but nobody answered. I called Victorine, but nobody was there. I called from the airport in Washington and the airport in Atlanta, then from the bus station in Atlanta and finally from the bus station in town, where I had left my car. I got Jason that time, who said that no, Helen wasn't home and yes, he would go to my house and look for her as soon as Helen's mother got home with the car.

I have no memory of the drive from the bus station home. It was dark by then, pitch dark. I do remember speeding up the hill, yet dreading what I would find. I have no idea whether the sun on the door was glowing, because I jumped out of the car and burst into the house, seeing nothing. I called Helen's house again, but nobody answered. I called Victorine, who said she would come at once. Oh, I needed her strength!

Then I got my flashlight and started toward the woods. The floodlight over the back steps lit the way for awhile, distorting the landscape with grotesque shadows. I felt that I was entering the timeless realm of my visions. Beyond the semi-circle of light, I slowed. I stopped. I could not—there was no way I could enter that darkness with nothing but a flashlight. A winter night creature screeched a warning. But love is a powerful ally. So I turned on my little beacon of light and, trembling, entered the woods.

It was quiet. There was peace here. But I feared what might be lurking in the dark. My flashlight found the path (the children's path), and I followed it to the cabin. In the shadows the cabin was no longer a ruin. The dark restored it to the sturdiness of the past, even to a kind of grandeur which comes to a thing that has defied time. I stopped, knowing that I could not go on.

Somewhere behind me I heard calls of "Miz Jenny! Miz Jenny!" and I knew that Victorine had come. Her presence gave me courage. I called once, "Here! Down here!" And I went through the empty doorway into the cabin.

Helen was there. My flashlight found her. In the thin light she seemed to be sleeping. She was curled up before the fireplace, knees to chest, her cheek resting on her arm.

And I wept. Thinking that if I had loved her more, if I had known more, if I had looked deeper into what I did know, if I had acted on what I thought I knew—oh, if! if! if! So I wept, because there was nothing left to do.

There was an autopsy. There was a physical reason for Helen's death—a congenital heart condition which her mother had not heeded. And evidences of abuse. (Oh, Helen!) For Jason was one in a series of "uncles" with whom Helen's mother, like other lonely women, filled the empty spaces in her life. I dare not even think of the load of guilt which that poor bewildered woman must bear. More than likely Helen would have gone anyway. This way, she went in peace. She went home, where she was wanted.

And finally, I, too, am at peace. I have written it all out, and now I know—I am not mad, nor was I ever mad. I came here fleeing the agony of loss—and found myself entangled in cosmic, timeless loss.

The past is never over. The past is one with the present, just as we, the we of now, are one with the future. We, if we are wise, learn from the past and hand the lessons, lovingly, to those who are yet to come.

Edward is not lost to me. Those years are part of what I am. And I must be about mending fences with my sons. For I am their past, and they are my future. And I must bring my grandchildren here, here to this mythic Southland, to learn its bitter lessons.

As for the cabin, I will leave it alone to finish its silent rotting away. It will lure nobody else. For Rachel has found her lost children.

# A Present for Sarah

I t cost a lot more than she had planned to spend for
Sarah's present. She was still learning to manage
on a pension—that and a pittance from a few small
investments—and so she was trying to be frugal. But
when she glanced into the window of Nanette's House
of Dolls, she was captivated by a sedate Victorian doll
house set on a stand in the corner, behind the festive
display of Santa's helpers in various elfin poses. There
it was, a veritable mansion in miniature, waiting to be
furnished and inhabited. She gripped her purse
tighter, as if it were a child struggling to get down.
Even on sale, the doll house cost more than she could
pay. But the mittens, hat and scarf set that she had
planned to buy for Sarah—a proper grandmotherly
gift—now seemed hopelessly drab, a dull practical
present that would hardly set nine-year-old eyes aglow.

Thanking God for credit cards, she hurried into
the shop. Minutes later, she emerged half-dragging
the heavy package, a replica of the model in the
window, which seemed to smile at her knowingly.
Now the twinkling lights and the flashy trees and
the poinsettias that brightened the mall lit within
her, for the first time this year, a feeling of
Christmas. A tentative feeling, which she didn't
entirely trust. So many times she had anticipated
joy, only to have her hopes vanish, to have the

memory of joyful anticipation bludgeon her into profound depression.

But the vision of Sarah opening her gift—*how in the world am I going to wrap it.*—warmed her so much that quite unconsciously she hummed along with the Christmas carols on her car radio all the way home. Sam will have to put the thing together, she thought with some apprehension. Shouldn't be too hard—no tools needed, the saleslady said. And in the middle of "Joy to the World" she remembered Sam as a little boy, screwdriver in hand, tinkering with some toy or other, his little face intent on his task. She blotted out the memory, crushed it, destroyed it, but suffered its bitter aftertaste even as she purged it from her mind.

They were going to let Sarah come and visit her on Christmas morning. Estelle would drop Sarah off, and Sam would pick her up an hour or so later, well before the elaborate Christmas dinner to which she—Sam's mother—was not, of course, invited. Well. At least she would see Sarah and give her a splendid present. Last year Estelle wouldn't permit even that. And Sam always supported Estelle's demands, no matter how perverted.

In front of her house, she braked too hard and grunted as the seat belt clutched her stomach. Pulling the awkward package up the front steps and into the living room, she muttered resolutely, "Not this time. Nothing's going wrong this time." Tossing her coat onto a chair, she hunted up some festive paper in which to wrap Sarah's gift.

Christmas morning dawned gray and threatening. Still, for her it held promise of a modicum of cheer. She would wait and open her presents with Sarah; it was no fun opening gifts by herself. Sarah's doll house, which she had finally managed to wrap, leaned against the wall in the alcove in the living room where numberless

Christmas trees had stood as the children were
growing up. And she slammed shut the door to her
memories. She tried—vainly—to keep out of her
heart the visions of all those Christmases, indelible
pictures of Christmas trees and stockings and the
children at different ages, and her parents—proud
grandparents themselves—and before that, she
herself and Melanie as little girls prancing down the
steps in that big old house chanting, "Hurrah!
Hurrah! Hurrah for Santa Claus!" And Frank.
Frank. Whose only share of Christmas now was the
wreath she laid on his grave.

She turned off the radio—no talk shows today,
only Christmas music—and started vacuuming and
tidying up. Sarah would be here directly.

Her daughter Cynthia called. All the way from
Brazil! Cynthia's two little boys came to the phone
and chattered about their presents and the party to
which they were going. Their grandmother warmed
her spirit at their voices as one warms her hands at
a fire, while the rest of the body remains in the chill
and the dark.

"Mom, how are you going to spend your day?"
Cynthia asked after the children had finished their
Christmas chat with Grandma.

"Sarah's coming over and later on I'm going to
Karen's for dinner. You haven't met Karen. She was
one of my students before I retired. She invited me
to dinner. "

"Oh, great." Cynthia sounded relieved. "So
Sarah's coming over? Estelle's going to let her come?"

"Estelle's bringing her."

"Have you heard from George?" Cynthia asked.

"Not yet. I guess he's working." George was her
youngest—an airline pilot, no less. He didn't call
often. But surely today....

"Well, Mom—say 'Hi' to everybody for me."

"Oh, sure. Love you, Mom. Take care."

"Love you, Cynthia."

Her eyes misted as she hung up the phone. She saw Cynthia as a little girl in braids, hugging a new Christmas doll. "Love you, Cynthia," she whispered again, hoping that despite the miles Cynthia would feel her love. Wishing that Cynthia's husband had not decided to accept the job in Brazil. Wishing.

She set her hands to doing last minute chores.

Eleven o'clock. She had thought that Sarah would be here by now. Eight o'clock in California. She would call her sister Melanie, wake her up maybe.

They talked for nearly half an hour. Funny, she thought, after all those years of feeling inferior to Melanie (the pretty one, the smart one, everyone had said), she felt so close to Melanie now. She wished they lived nearer to one another. Wished.

Twelve o'clock. Morning was over. She stopped trying to pretend away her anxiety and sat by the window to watch for Estelle's car. To watch for Sarah. Gazing out at the winter street, she wondered again how her relationship with her son's family had gotten so painful.

She knew now that Estelle had never liked her—had, in fact, hated her ever since Sam had brought his pretty little bride home to meet his mother. Estelle's past was a mystery; nobody had ever mentioned her family, her girlhood, even her home town. Sam had met Estelle when he was stationed in South Carolina, that was all that anybody knew, and when he was discharged from the Army, Estelle came home with him. It was soon evident that something was dreadfully wrong: Estelle drank too much, talked too loud, lost her temper over nothing, lied compulsively, and after a period of armed truce with Sam's increasingly disapproving family, cursed

them out separately and collectively. And Sam said
nothing, but he became more and more alienated
from his people, especially his mother.

Estelle had particularly hated her ever since the
night of the family reunion, when she had blundered
into a dark hallway and discovered Estelle with
Sam's young cousin embracing, locked together with
his hand under her dress. Estelle's startled glance,
the cousin's sheepish look, and her own
embarrassment as she backed away as if she, rather
than they, had transgressed, remained a permanent
record in her memory. She had never told Sam of his
wife's treachery, but from that moment Estelle had
made a conscious and obvious effort to discredit and
belittle her mother-in-law in every possible way.

And now, years later, Sam's mother sat alone
waiting. The seconds ticked by, and the minutes
passed, and her unopened presents in their garish
wrappings mocked her, and the big box leaned
saucily against the wall in the alcove where the
Christmas trees had once stood.

At one o'clock she called. No answer. Maybe they
were on their way here.

At three she dressed to go out for dinner. At four
she left. And the Christmas cheer at Karen's house
nearly melted the frozen tears she held inside.
Karen's husband and little girl, Karen's mother,
Karen's friends embraced her and honored her. And
she was grateful. But there was a bottomless well
inside her self which nothing could fill.

At nine, home again, she called. Estelle
answered. Loud music, raucous laughter in the
background.

"Oh—we were running late—Sarah had things to
do—" Estelle's words were slurred. "Maybe one day
next week—"

At ten she made herself a drink, extra strong this time, and by ten-thirty her Christmas was over.

---

The holidays passed and winter set in. On icy days she was glad that she no longer had to go to work. Her bones had thinned with the passing years, and the thought of a fall on ice terrified her. Still, when it snowed she shoveled her sidewalk herself because there was nobody to do it. She had always been proud of her independence, but now she was beginning to wonder how much longer she could carry on alone and who would help her when she faltered.

The days passed slowly. Mornings from her window she watched the bustle of people going to work, and as she sipped her tea, she missed her job, especially her students. Sometimes she laced her tea with rum and spent the next hour or two in a soft glow. On sunny days she shopped, lunched out, then came home and wrote letters or read. Sometimes she had a meal with a friend—but by now many of her friends had passed on, and the ones left were in dubious health. Evenings she sipped wine or scotch and nodded in front of the TV. Each day she resolved not to drink that night, but the long dark brought an unacknowledged terror, and she embraced the bottle as she would have embraced a friend. Sitting alone in that house where so many had lived, she sipped. Her spirit slumbered in a soft cocoon of booze. Then one night after three drinks she caught sight of her flushed face in the mirror. And what resolution couldn't do, disgust did.

What does one do with an undelivered Christmas gift? It stood against the wall long after she had put away the lights and the wreath. It was too big to fit into anywhere easily. She moved it from one place to another, but wherever she put it, it stayed a constant reminder of Sam's and Estelle's perfidy.

Finally, in frustration she began tearing off the paper in which she had so carefully wrapped it. Tore it off furiously, balled it up, pounded it into a shapeless mass of crumpled snowmen and jingle bells, and flung it into the trash can. But she didn't feel any better. Shorn of its gaudy covering, the unwieldy box looked all the more menacing. One day, coming in from shoveling snow, her hands stinging and her back aching, she caught sight of the big box and simply sat down and cried.

Cried for the three little children who had grown up and flown from her—Cynthia to Brazil, George to the skyways of the world, Sam to a neurotic wife—removing themselves from her life and effectively keeping her out of theirs. Cried for the children who had grown into adults whom she hardly knew. What was her girl to her now but a voice on the telephone, and how many months had it been since Georgie bothered to call her? And Sam, just outside of town, Sammy of the twinkling eyes and ready grin, who never called, never stopped over to see about her—When did her children die, and who were these people who called themselves Cynthia and George and Sam?

The storm of tears was brief, but the depression that followed was a fog that blanketed her afternoon.

As evening approached, she finally stopped her restless wandering from room to empty room and settled in the den, where she found herself staring at the box which seemed to embody the agony of her alienation from her children. Perhaps the glow of dusk wove an air of mystery about the room, or perhaps the residue of tears softened her vision. But the box seemed strangely inviting, as if it held comfort inside, even, perhaps, joy. She had never had a doll house as a child, and the big old Victorian mansion was somehow like the home she had imagined for herself a long time ago. It was a place where she, like the heroines in her fairy tales, could live happily ever after.

On an impulse she opened the box. *All those parts! Lord, how do they expect folks to make sense out of that?* She'd never been good at putting things together, but the challenge intrigued her. *Let's see—a screwdriver, that's all I need...*and squinting to read the tiny print, she began to figure out the directions, which seemed to be written in English translated from some other language by an inept translator. Step by step, she began to fit together the walls and floors. It was not as easy as the saleslady had said. But by now she was committed to the task. She made mistakes, had to go back and puzzle over the instructions, muttered a few "damns." Hours passed, but she did not stop to fix supper. Finally she got everything right. And there it was! She got up stiffly and backed across the room to see it from a distance. She smiled, pleased.

There was something familiar about the house. Deep within some area of her self, she had seen it before.

———————————

The frigid weather continued. The snow was piled into dirty gray mounds, and patches of ice rose like ugly scars on streets and sidewalks. She tried to keep busy, but housework had always bored her, and telephone conversations with her cronies were merely islands in the bottomless ocean of her loneliness. There was no need for any pattern to her days. There was nobody to be affected by anything she might do. She had thought that in her retirement she would travel—go and see some of the places she had read about. But travel costs money, and she was afraid to tap her small savings. Besides, she was beginning to be plagued by a bit of forgetfulness and was fearful of traveling alone. She was no hermit: she went to lectures, did volunteer work as a tutor, and spent hours at the library. But whatever she did, she could not somehow stay ahead of the loneliness that continued to dog her steps. She existed on the rim of life rather than within its core. She had the feeling that if she were suddenly to disappear, nobody would notice. In her golden years she had run out of dreams.

More and more she was drawn to the doll house. It was a sturdy, three-story structure with an ornate front. The back was completely open, and all the rooms, hallways, and staircases were visible. Three rooms of furniture had come with the house: bedroom, living room, and kitchen. Carefully she unwrapped each tiny piece and set it in place. The bed went there, where sunlight would flow upon it from the front window; the bureau here on the opposite wall; the chest of drawers farther along the same wall. Downstairs the sofa went here....

And so she passed a winter afternoon, arranging and rearranging doll furniture. Dusk had fallen by the time she finished. She was pleased with her work— the rooms looked real. But there were still seven empty rooms. She was repelled by the emptiness; it made her restless, even fearful. She turned the open side of the house to the wall. But the dignified front could not disguise the fact that the beautiful exterior hid emptiness inside.

As soon as she could get out, she went back to Nanette's House of Dolls. She chose carefully. *Mercy! Who would have thought they'd cost so much!* Another bedroom—a child's this time and, let's see, a dining room, a den with comfortable overstuffed chairs. And, oh yes, a bathroom with all the necessary facilities. Lovely, old-fashioned things.

The saleslady for some reason remembered her. "I'll bet that little girl of yours is having a ball with her doll house."

"Oh yes." she lied, handing over her credit card. Yet perhaps she didn't really lie. For the little girl within her was nourished by the doll house, was coming alive again.

And now her need to finish the doll house was compelling. She made repeated trips to Nanette's and other toy stores. There was no end to the furnishings to be found. She created a third bedroom, another bath, and a library with great tall bookcases, an old-fashioned typewriter, and even a ponderous desk like the one Papa had had in the big old house where she and Melanie had grown up. And a stand with an unabridged dictionary!

Finally the house was complete. All the rooms were furnished. But still she was unsatisfied.

March was cruel that year. Even as the days passed, it held no promise of spring. Sleet and freezing rain immobilized the city and kept the elderly housebound.

One day she decided to do a task which she had postponed for ages: she would go through the old photographs and put them into the albums she had bought years ago and never used. She exhumed all the pictures from the various drawers in which they had been so carelessly tossed and began to assemble them on the kitchen table.

The task was unexpectedly painful. For scattered before her, in a profusion of memories, were all the people who had mattered in her life, even her own past selves, all smiling at her, all tormenting her with their innocence of the pain that awaited them in future years—all lost and gone and ever present.

Here were Mama and Papa holding the infant Sammy, their first grandchild, and proudly smiling. They were vigorous and youthful. How could they know of the years to come, Papa's body eaten away by cancer, Mama's mind eroded by senility? And here she was herself, she and Melanie, little girls. She was clinging to Big Sister's hand, shrinking timidly from the camera, a bright bow-ribbon on her hair. Melanie was smiling confidently, as well she might: Melanie was beautiful in her new Easter frock and patent leather baby-doll shoes.

And here was Frank—her Frank. Her hand trembled, because he was standing beside the new car, a grin lighting his face like a halo. The new car they had planned for so carefully—and now here it was. The car in which three years later Frank would be mangled beyond recognition, that night when he should have been home but was out drinking, drinking with that woman who was pulled with him from the wreckage, joined with him forever in death. Frank! Her Frank! She dropped that photograph as if it scorched her fingers, buried it on the bottom of the pile, hastily pulled out another picture.

A rather formal picture, carefully posed. The children, Sammy and Cynthia on either side of her, smiling woodenly, and the baby Georgie fat and goggle-eyed on her lap. Frank was not in the picture; he was behind the camera. Looking deeply into her former self's smile, she felt that she had never been that happy woman. Felt disconnected from her. Where had the years gone? And why was she sitting alone in this empty house poring through dog-eared pictures?

She dumped them into a plastic bag and re-interred them in a bureau drawer. For a few minutes she crouched on the floor beside the bureau, her eyes closed, her hands balled into fists, trying to shut out the present and find her way back to the past, as if she could relive her life and somehow alter it so that this present time, this now would never come.

Then she got up and went into the den, as if the doll house had drawn her there. For a moment or two she looked steadily at the big old Victorian house with all the furniture. Then she smiled. No wonder the doll house seemed empty. Nobody lived there.

She would bring it a family.

She felt a surge of joy as she fingered the miniature dolls at Nanette's—an eerie sense of beginning again. The dolls were so beautifully wrought—almost like little people in her hands. She wouldn't have been surprised if they had begun to squirm and wriggle to get loose.

She chose carefully. *Let's see—a mother and a father—no, not that mother; she's too—oh, too something or other, not really right somehow—*And so she went, picking and choosing and rejecting. The children would be most difficult. What sort of children would the doll family have? Two little girls, that would be nice. She went to three different malls and then back to Nanette's a second time before she could make her selections. On a sudden whim she bought a boy doll, too, one nearly as tall as the mother. She had always wanted a big brother, and now the doll girls would have one.

It was a cruel coincidence or perhaps a sally of fate that she came home to news of another death. Mary Esther, her friend since elementary school. Mary Esther!

The news was not unexpected nor even, in a sense, unwelcome, for Mary Esther had been failing for months now, her body shrunken, her face unrecognizable. But death is always a shock, and the tense voice of Mary Esther's son on the answering machine did not have to say the dread words. His anguish alone told all there was to tell.

There were the usual calls to Mary Esther's family and to the few remaining friends. And beneath her grief for her girlhood companion pulsed the thought, "There's hardly anyone left who remembers me as a child."

By eight o'clock the calls had all been made, and still there seemed no way to assuage her grief. She called Melanie, but nobody was at home, and she could not get a call through to Cynthia in Brazil. She turned on the television but could not stand the slick posturing on the tube. Her loneliness deepened.

Then she remembered the doll family. She would while away the time before sleep by setting the dolls in place. She sat down in front of the table on which the Victorian structure rested. Yes, the house was just right. She had put a sheet of green construction paper under it—green like a wide green lawn. For this house was in the suburbs, not right in the middle of the city like the big row house of her own childhood, and nobody but the family would live in the doll house—no roomers to rent the upstairs rooms so that Papa could meet the mortgage.

Carefully, she put Mama in the kitchen, where she would prepare luscious meals—and she would like taking care of the family, would never have to go out to a job she hated and come home exhausted and irritable—because this Papa made enough money to give them everything they needed. Now, Papa—let's see, she put Papa in the library right beside the desk where he could read or work, and he was happy. The boy doll—she named him Eric—she put in the den. She would get him a telephone—one of the old-fashioned upright phones—so that he could talk with his friends.

The two little girls. What would she name them? She thought, unconsciously drawing her brows together in the frown that had put a furrow between her eyes.

She named the bigger doll Marjorie, after herself. This time Marjorie would be the older. Marjorie would be the pretty one, the confident one.

But the tiny girl— Melanie, of course—would be pretty, too. Marjorie would take care of her, even when Melanie was something of a pest. She put little Melanie in the bedroom, where she could play with her toys. Marjorie, of course, she put in the library with Papa, where she could sit in the big chair and read all those shelves of books and write poems on the typewriter.

She sat back, looked over the doll family, and smiled. Yes, they were just right. Her eyes lingered especially over Mama and Papa. Yes. He would always be strong and vigorous and would never spend his last days struggling for breath and begging for those deadly cigarettes. And Mama would be gentle and loving, never harsh, and she would love Marjorie as much as she did Melanie, and never, never forget her daughter Marjorie and end up calling her Melanie even though the real Melanie had long since moved across the country and only Marjorie was there to hear.

Hardly a day passed when she did not sit at the table and watch the doll family's activities. She moved them about in their grand Victorian house as they interacted with one another and played out their little dramas. Sometimes the children quarreled with one another or pouted over some trifle—Eric did not like mowing the huge lawn, and Melanie did not want to pick up her toys—but the infinite patience and wisdom of Mama and Papa soon restored harmony.

Sometimes she bought them some new household furnishing—a swing set for the children, a sewing machine for Mama—and they were delighted. One day she went to buy a playmate for the girls. Spring had come by now, and the sun's gentle warmth had awakened within her a dormant joy. Striding through the mall, she glimpsed her reflection in a store window. Usually she avoided these chance encounters with her self: she never felt her age, and the image which peered so warily back at her seemed to be that of some older woman who was somehow wearing her clothes. But today was different. Her reflection was that of a vital young woman, her step meaningful and definite, a woman sure of her place in life.

She found a perky little girl doll with a mischievous grin. A great companion for Marjorie. She named the new doll Mary Esther.

Watching the dolls that night and listening to their chatter, she had a comfortable feeling of finally being home after a long and arduous journey.

---

The quarrel with Estelle was unexpected and devastating. The jangle of the telephone shocked her out of an uneasy slumber.

"Marjorie—" Estelle had long since stopped calling her Mom—"What are you into? Aunt Melanie just called us and said she hasn't been able to reach you, and you haven't answered her letters. Where have you been?"

The question was an accusation. Had she been fully awake, she might have answered more diplomatically. She had always censored what she said to Estelle.

"Well, if you gave a shit you'd know," she heard herself saying—incredulously she heard herself saying that to Estelle.

Her daughter-in-law's tidal wave of words sizzled the telephone lines. By the time she was actually awake, she heard only wisps of Estelle's tirade "...crazy old woman...think I'm not good enough...stay away from Sarah...bitch...bitch..."

Awake now, she shrieked into the phone obscenities she had forgotten that she knew, and for a few seconds Estelle screamed back, and the two of them harmonized in a duet of hate. Then for several minutes she continued in a terrible solo, until the dial tone finally told her that her passion was being wasted.

All that morning she defiled her silent house with rage. She banged doors, flung silverware into the sink, stamped from room to room, and still could not lessen her rage—rage for all the years when her firstborn had sold out his family for the love of a fool. Beneath her rage she sheltered a forlorn hope that Sam would call her and somehow make things right. But hours passed and Sam never called.

The old depression settled around her. She felt like an old broom that for too many years had been dragged through other people's dirt.

By afternoon, unable to stand the dissonance of her silent house, she went out to the shopping mall where there were hordes of people. She was able to eat a little lunch, and then, reluctant to go home, she meandered among the shops. Her feet took her into Nanette's.

She would make a new family.

That evening her frantic fingers put the new family in place. Mama and Papa became Marjorie and Frank—right for each other now. The Eric doll became Sam, the oldest child, and the former Marjorie doll became Cynthia. There was now a toddler Georgie, who lived in what had become the nursery.

The family dynamics changed. Marjorie now went out daily to a career which she loved, not because she had to—for Frank supported them adequately—but because she loved her work and had something to contribute. Frank and the children pitched in to help with the house work, and they all lived joyously. And nobody grew up, and nobody was unfaithful, and the world yielded her heart's desire.

The April rains came and went, and this year she did not plant her garden. She seldom went out now, but devoted most of her time to the doll family. She found some toy trees and placed them in the right places in the doll yard, and she cut out some flowers from a seed catalogue and pasted them around the base of the house. She bought two toy cars—one for Marjorie and one for Frank—so that they could go on errands and visits to friends.

Now and then necessity drove her out to the bank and the supermarket. She was aware then that the mail was accumulating. She had long since— the day after the quarrel with Estelle—taken her phone off the hook. She no longer prepared meals; she nibbled whatever was there now and then to relieve hunger. Her body went through the necessary routines of toilet and sleeping. Most days she forgot to dress or comb her hair. Most nights she slept on the rug in the den.

The doll family became the center of her life. They were everything that she wanted them to be, and her waking hours were devoted to them. Gradually it dawned on her that the dolls had a life of their own, independent of her. Sometimes when she dozed curled up on the rug (for by now she no longer went to bed at all), she would awaken to find the dolls in different places from where she had left them. They were moving about when she wasn't watching: things were happening to them that she didn't even know about.

When she gazed at them their tiny upturned faces seemed to beseech her, and their little arms were open in a silent plea. Sometimes in the dark she would hear the tinkle of little doll voices.

"What—what?" one night she whispered into the darkness. Moonlight and the glow of street lamps flowed into the room, and the headlights of passing cars made the shadows come alive, so that the room and everything in it seemed to be moving, whirling, caught up in a macabre dance. The doll house was the center of the dance, and as it swayed and gyrated, it compelled her toward it and she was sucked into the whirlpool.

"God!" she cried out in a final moment of lucidity, as she sank to her knees.

---

And then it was daylight, and she was strolling up the walk toward the front door. Night rain had washed the air clean, and the sun sparkled on the gleaming house. The flowers were gorgeous that morning, dazzling splashes of red and orange and gold. And look—a butterfly! The grass needed cutting, though. She would have to get Sammy on the job, like it or not. She smiled.

They were all at the door to meet her. "Hey, Mom, where you been?" asked the Sammy doll, hugging her, grinning. "Love you, Mom," said the Cynthia doll, standing back a little, her eyes shining. "Mommy! Mommy!" cried the Georgie doll, hugging her around the legs. She laughed aloud—it had been so long since she had laughed out of sheer joy! And when the children had gone out into the yard, the Frank doll came to her and embraced her. And his gentle touch found all the hungry places.

From that moment she was the Marjorie doll, a woman fulfilled in all her roles, warmed by her loving family, never making any mistakes and never having any reason to cry.

She did not hear the insistent door chimes nor, later, the smashing of a window. She did not hear Sam's explosive "Oh my God!" as he plunged into the room; she did not even hear his shouts, "Mom! Mom!" She did cringe when he dropped to his knees on the floor beside her, where she lay curled like a child unborn. Her eyes slid open when he shook her, and she managed to focus them upon a distraught

A Present for Sarah

Estelle, standing over her and screaming, "Well, Goddammit, what the hell is wrong with her?" She vaguely heard Sam snap, *"Shut up, Estelle she's my mother!"* And for a moment she felt herself cradled in protecting arms.

Then Marjorie closed her eyes again and sank back into the deepest recesses of her self.

They could not know these strangers who would pry her out of her real world—that she had plumbed her depths and that she knew who and what she was. And that she was really quite content.

147

# *Journey Through Woods*

**"L**ord, Little Gene, you sure done got heavy,"
Azuree murmured to the child in her arms, not
in a complaining tone but rather with an air of
wonderment. The sleeping child lay limp, his skinny
little legs flopping against her as she trudged. She
paused a moment and shifted his weight. She laid
his cheek on her shoulder and folded her arms under
his small behind. His arms dangled dismally as she
resumed her walk. They were an odd sight, almost
an impurity on the pristine woods. She was a gaunt
woman in early middle age. Her skirt and blouse
were wrinkled, and her short Afro was unkempt.

Azuree smiled deep down inside. "You all right
now," she whispered to the child. All those years of
lonely struggle, years of not knowing, of trying
everything and failing, of desperation and fear—all
those years. And now it was over. The decision was
finally made. She pressed him tightly to her breast,
as if her love were strong enough to heal them both.
A profound peace had descended upon her, softly like
a cloud drifting earthward. Without conscious
volition, she began to hum and then to sing the
words, "...*steal away to Jesus. I ain't got long to stay
here. . .*"

Scent of pine and wildflowers sweetened the air, and birds chirped and twittered their praise songs. She raised her eyes for a moment. The trees spread their leafy branches above her in lacy profusion. Sunshine poured through the breaks in the branches, and here and there she glimpsed deep blue cloudless sky. The ground was soft beneath her feet, cushioned by generations of fallen leaves. Somewhere there was honeysuckle; its scent brought back the springtimes of her childhood when she, Junie and Joetta used to pick the fragrant blossoms and suck the sweet juice. *"The trumpet sounds within-a my soul.... "* She smiled and then she sighed. She would have to sit down and rest. *"Steal away, steal away...,"* she crooned. *"Steal away home..., "* and suddenly she stopped singing. She could not remember the words. For where was home? In all this world, where now was home?

She stopped walking, momentarily confused. She knew that she was bone-tired and weakened from lack of food and sleep. She laid the child carefully on a mossy bed and knelt beside him, gazing at his peaceful face. "You all right now, honey," she murmured. "You all right now." She couldn't stop saying it, repeated it compulsively, sobbing, until her voice rose to a scream and her words tumbled into each other. And, then, she stopped screaming, and the world was silent, and she heard nothing—no birdsong, no rustling of leaves. Nothing. And she stared in horror at the sleeping child, whom no sound would ever awaken.

They had spent last night in a barn on the fringe of the woods. She had carried the child carefully as one would carry a crystal goblet. On her back was a bulky red backpack containing everything they would need. She had flung a long black shawl over that, so that as she struggled under the weight of her various burdens, she resembled a hunchback struggling up a hill.

Dusk had fallen by the time she set Little Gene down and pushed open the heavy door. The setting sun cast lurid shadows and nothing resembled its daylight self. She picked up the child and entered the barn's twilight world, lit by the dying sun and pungent with the odor of animals. A startled "moooo" from nearby set her frightened heart to racing. She clutched Little Gene again to her breast. The child apparently felt no fear, for he neither trembled nor cried aloud but met this world with the same indifference with which he regarded everything else, neither crying nor smiling, as if nothing outside of his body were actually real. His indifference gave her courage, and as her eyes became accustomed to the darkness, she made out the shadowy forms of a cow and a calf confined in a stall, staring uneasily at the newcomers. Smiling at her own uneasiness, she spread out her shawl on the floor. She laid the child down and changed his diaper, glad that she had had the foresight to put some clean ones into the backpack. She groped in the dark, wishing she had thought to bring a flashlight. For the hundredth time that day, her fingers touched the little bottle in her skirt pocket, assuring her that the bottle was still there. Over by the cow's stall she found a trough full of sweet hay. She spread her shawl over the hay, and reverently, she laid the child upon it. He was soon asleep.

All night she kept a solitary vigil, dozing now and then but mostly thinking, remembering. Wrestling to subdue those thoughts that would come to destroy her newfound peace.

She thought about Melvin and tried unsuccessfully to repress the hurt. Where was he now? she wondered, and did he ever think about her and their son? No way, she thought bitterly. *Bastard wouldn't give us the time of day. Just up and left us, just up and left.* Five years, five years since he left. Just left one morning going to work, he said. But evening came, and night fell, and morning came again, and Melvin never showed. She did wonder how he had managed to smuggle his clothes from the closet without her knowledge. *Guess that was the one smart thing he ever done in his miserable life.* In this long night of agonized waiting, that other night returned to her as sharp as a razor—that night when she had sat at the kitchen table staring at her half empty coffee cup, sloshing the cold coffee around in nervous circles, waiting for Melvin and knowing that she was utterly alone.

Now, in the quiet barn, she turned to Little Gene and stroked his hair. He sighed in his sleep. "Poor little lamb," she murmured. "Poor little lamb." The cow lowed in her stall, and the calf gave a contented sigh.

Suddenly she panicked. She scrambled to her feet and stared wildly around the barn in which nothing was visible. Her heart beat crazily, and her breath came in labored spurts. Overcome by weakness, she sank to her knees. God! She had to get herself together.

Gradually, the panic passed. But she still trembled, and she still felt weak as water. Oh—she realized that she had not eaten all day and, in fact, had eaten next to nothing in the past several days as she wrestled with her indecision. That morning at breakfast in the hospital the watery scrambled eggs had sickened her. She had choked down a mouthful or two, but her stomach churned, and the eggs had slid wretchedly back into her soggy napkin. Nobody noticed. She wrapped her roll in a fresh napkin, to tide her over until the next meal, if necessary, and then fled.

Later, preparing for her journey, she had fished the hardened roll out of her pocket and stuffed it into the backpack. "I guess that's it," she muttered. She took one more look into each room—bleak, scantily furnished, cold. Empty as if nobody had ever lived there. But these rooms had been hers, and they had been home. At the kitchen she paused. Unbidden, the tears came. And the kitchen blurred and wavered, and in its softness, it looked lush and inviting.

She wiped away the tears and took one hard look around to see if she had forgotten anything Oh—there on the table was a Chianti bottle with a finger of wine still left, glowing richly red in the sunshine. Later on her strength would surely need bolstering. She poured the wine into a small mayonnaise jar and pushed it into the backpack. Then she turned and left without looking back.

Now, crouching on the straw-strewn floor of the barn, she munched the dried up roll. But her mouth was so dry that the bread stuck in her throat, and she washed it down with a swallow of Chianti. The tension began to unravel. She was soothed.

She whisked various little piles of hay together and made herself a bed next to the trough where Little Gene slept. She must sleep—tomorrow would require all her strength. But memories were too loud to let her rest.

Melvin, when she first knew him, was an orderly at Saint Simon's where she had just gotten a job as a nurse's aid. Her first job since she had defied Junie and Joetta and moved to the city. Hard work, but something in her was satisfied taking care of folks. *Seem like that's all I ever done, take care of somebody, mostly somebody that couldn't even say thanks.* And for a moment her thoughts left Melvin and turned to her earliest days. Huh! *Joetta the oldest, two years older than me. How come I always got the chores ? They used to say Joetta looked just like Mama 'fore she married Pa and worked all that prettiness away. Wonder who do I look like. Don't make no never mind, I guess. I still got all the chores.*

In spite of herself, a tear slipped out of her closed eyes. She must be extra sensitive because of what she was going to have to do tomorrow. She reached over and touched Little Gene's warm hair, soft to her touch. She wrapped the shawl closer around him. She touched the little bottle in her skirt pocket.

Memories crowded in on her. *And that damned Junie,* she thought, but strangely enough without rancor. Junie was just a year younger, but somehow she was always the one responsible for him. *Take your brother's hand...why'd you let him fall down them stairs...how come you let him go outside by hisself—he coulda got lost somewheres....* And even later, when Joetta had married—what was his name? No matter, he didn't last long, and Junie had babies scattered all over the county. Somehow, she was always the one who cleaned up after Joetta and Junie, taking over the care of little Clarence, whom Joetta had had at sixteen by some no-account boy, until Joetta married two years later and snatched the baby from her, and then later on, dropped off Clarence and the other babies who had come for Azuree to take care of while she, Joetta, good-timed her way through life.

Azuree reached up and patted Little Gene.

Mama. Her image came with frightening clarity. The long months of sickness and pain when Mama refused to see a doctor, and only Azuree could stay with her and nurse her and see the breast she had suckled grow swollen and discolored as the poison worked its way through Mama's body. In her coffin, Mama had looked young and pretty again, a faint smile on her lips, as if in death she had discovered the secret of life. And then, Papa finding his comfort in the bottle and God knows what else, until that stormy night when he wandered from the tavern lost and drunk in the cold rain. By the time he had sobered up and managed to find his way home it was too late. He was hot with fever, and no doctor could help him. Even after he stopped talking at all, his hot eyes accused Azuree because she didn't know how to perform miracles.

Well. Melvin. So there she was at Saint Simon's. Joetta and Junie had both felt that Mama's and Papa's home was still theirs, and there they dropped off their problems. At first she had been glad of their company, because with Papa and Mama both gone, she didn't know what to do with her life, so she kept up the decrepit little house and received gladly Joetta's children when Joetta was between marriages, and Junie himself when his current wife threw him out. She found herself a job in a tobacco factory. But one day in a flash of insight, she realized that her life was a desert, and she was a lost and lonely traveler. So in a moment of rare courage, she took what insurance money was left, and without saying goodbye to anyone, she caught the bus for the nearest big city. All the way, without a notion of what her new life would be like, she felt for the first time, free.

Saint Simon's. Melvin. Tall, light-skinned, with those haunting gray eyes and that wavy hair, which he was fond of combing as they were leaving for the movies or for a walk in the park. And most especially as he was leaving her apartment after an evening of watching TV and snuggling on the sofa. Out of the corner of her eye, she would catch him glancing in the mirror and giving his hair a quick, self-satisfied swipe with the comb.

There wasn't any grand romance. She and Melvin had drifted together, and when he left his job at the hospital, they had kept seeing each other. It wasn't that they were deeply in love—only that neither had anybody else. For she was timid and plain, someone whom people never really noticed, and Melvin, though mildly nice-looking, lacked the strength of character that makes a man memorable. They were both invisible people. Sex occurred, not through any great passion, but because it was the natural next step, and neither had the fortitude to resist it or even make it interesting. And when she came up pregnant, they married—an unnecessary inconvenience, because in the fifth month she miscarried, and the baby girl died without ever having lived. Huddling in the sparse hay, Azuree shivered and the memories came thick and fast like gnats in the afternoon sun.

Another year, another miscarriage. *Good thing, she told herself then and reiterated now, Melvin didn't have no job, and I had to carry all the load. What was I gonna do with a baby?* But even now, when tears came so insistently, she wished that the baby had lived, wished that her body had nurtured that baby instead of destroying it. Anyway, the marriage had plodded on, and in its very dullness she found security.

Melvin was pleasant and easy to please. He demanded little and gave little. He never seemed to be *present*, even when they made love, even at the climactic moment when he cried out something incomprehensible, even then he seemed not to be there. Or perhaps *he* was there, and she wasn't.

One by one, he took her to meet his brothers and sisters—three of each. Melvin was their baby, on whom they all doted. They called him "Baby Brother" and treated him with a strange sort of reverence, as if their hopes for eternal redemption lay in him. And he glowed in their admiration, and with them he was beautiful, and with them he was whole.

None of them particularly liked Azuree. She sensed it at once with each of them. For all except— what was her name? —had married people who were lighter-skinned than they were. Washing the race clean, old folks used to say. And no matter how hard she tried to be agreeable or how good a wife she was, Melvin's brothers and sisters never forgave her for being browner than they, and darker than Melvin, who was the lightest of them all.

Azuree never confided in Melvin her feelings about his family.

He accepted life as it appeared, never probing from his family's bright greetings to their hidden antipathy toward his wife. Azuree found excuses for not accompanying him on his frequent visits, and after awhile he stopped inviting her. He went alone, and none of them ever visited Melvin's home. For awhile Azuree was silently resentful. But in time Melvin's relatives—and eventually Melvin himself—took their places in the gray area that contained those who no longer mattered.

Even now she tried not to think of—the other one. The intern whose name she had managed to forget. But before she could shut down her heart, he came to her even in this dark place on this fateful night. The sight of his smooth brown skin and laughing eyes, the scent of him, the sound of his whisper, the feel of his hardness thrusting into her softness. The feeling of being gloriously, gloriously alive.

Gary, yes, that was his name, Gary Knight. He was assigned to oncology, where Azuree carried bedpans, bathed ravished bodies, distributed comfort where she could, and tried to smooth the pathway to death. When she first came to St. Simon's, she worked in maternity, where life began. In some way the new little lives gave her faith in life's infinite possibilities. She would pause sometimes and gaze through the window of the nursery, and in her heart she would bless the tiny babies. Azuree loved the glow on the faces of the mothers—some of the mothers—when they held their babies and suckled them. But she could not repress a spontaneous feeling of envy because her own almost-babies had ended up as garbage.

The transfer to oncology revealed what was apparently her real mission in life—to ease the way of the doomed. Azuree rejoiced whenever a patient left the hospital with hope revived, life reaffirmed. But it was the hopeless whose flickering lives gave meaning to hers. It was she to whom they confided their fears, she to whom they made their final confessions, she to whose hand they clung when they faced the dread moment.

In the midst of all that death came Gary Knight. Tall, slender, and the color of sweet hot chocolate, with just a touch of melted marshmallow. He hardly noticed her except to nod a greeting as they passed in the corridors or in patients' rooms. But Azuree, restless in a moribund marriage, noticed him. Fantasies came unbidden at the oddest moments, and in her weekly (Saturdays usually) sex with Melvin, she fantasized that it was Gary who lay upon her, and the hot gushes of passion came, to Melvin's surprised delight.

The Taylor boy's death brought her and Gary together. The boy was nine years old. Leukemia. They watched together, Azuree and Gary, she holding his hand, Gary speaking softly to him and stroking his hair. When the parents came, Azuree and Gary withdrew. But both were shaken.

"I thought he was going to make it—at least for a while," Gary muttered.

And now they were comforting each other. "You not supposed to get, you know, so much into patients that you get hurt," she told him. She was thirty-eight to his twenty-something. In spite of their differences in status at the hospital, she felt like his comforter, his protector. After that, they had special smiles for each other, and now and then they would share a table in the cafeteria. Little by little she learned him—his wife Estelle's impatience with their poverty, his interest in psychiatry although he didn't want to study that long, his parents' dire need and his dilemma whether to quit and get a job or to continue the hard way of his medical training. It never occurred to Azuree to tell him about her tottering marriage, her estrangement from her brother and sister, her daily little struggles to know who she was and where, if anywhere, she was bound.

It was an easy step from the cafeteria to his room.

And then—nothing. In the corridors, in patients' rooms, in the cafeteria he was again a stranger, never speaking to her, never smiling, never even seeing her as she passed. For awhile she was stunned. Then she began seeing him having lunch and spending spare moments with Linda Schwartzmann, a hospital social worker who was young, pretty, and white.

Azuree turned to Melvin with a passion that startled and intimidated him. Night after night for nearly a month she gave him no peace, pushing his slack lips to her breast, wrapping her legs around him, fondling his flaccid penis until it hardened, and then mounting him and riding him like a surfer on stormy seas. And afterward, after the clutching and the crying out and the spasm, when they lay exhausted, she teetered on the edge of her side of the bed, as far from him as she could get, and her silent tears were a sad counterpoint to his fervent snores.

At the end of the month, her breasts were heavy and tender, and no blood came.

Now, in the moon-haunted barn, Azuree shivered. She fingered the bottle in her pocket. She took Little Gene from the trough and wrapped him more snugly in her shawl. She pressed him close to her and tried to draw a modicum of warmth from his thin body. He sighed in his sleep but remained remote from her need.

She tried with all her strength to slam the door of memory. Tried to forget Gary's startled face when she told him that she was pregnant, then his obvious avoidance of her and finally his transfer out of oncology. Tried to forget the agony of waiting all those months and wondering whom the child would favor. Tried to forget her anxious searching of the child's face, then the conclusion that he was the image of herself, as if she alone had created him. Now, on their bed of hay, she hugged the child hard, warmed him with her desperation. Little Gene sighed again and snuggled close to her. And what was animal instinct, her starved self mistook for love.

She slept fitfully, and her waking moments were haunted by memories. The baby had been her world. Melvin had named him Eugene after the oldest brother, the one who had money. Azuree had plunged into motherhood as one would plunge into a sea of healing waters. Her pleasure was bathing and dressing the baby, then feeding him the rich milk from her breast and rocking him until they both fell asleep.

When Melvin came home from work (at a sleazy restaurant, where, at 36, he was a bus boy), she was too tired and too preoccupied for much conversation. If Melvin expected a return of her passion, he was terribly disappointed. Now, in the dark barn, she squirmed uncomfortably and turned over on her back. She did not want to think of those days.

In spite of all her care, Little Gene had failed to thrive. Scrawny from the beginning, he was slow to develop. He seldom cried and never smiled; he just lay in his crib and stared vacantly at the ceiling. As the months passed, he remained as undeveloped as a newborn—he never learned to turn over, sit up alone, wave bye-bye, feed himself. He never even babbled as babies do before learning to speak. He was content to lie where Azuree put him, regarding her and Melvin and the ceiling with the same vacant gaze. Azuree took him to the clinic faithfully every month. And now the tears came copiously, as she remembered that awful moment when there was no hiding place from the truth, when she sat clutching little Gene as the doctor told her "...severely retarded...institution...never live a normal life...never live...never live..."

She tried hard not to remember the horror of those days, her frantic prayers and then the bitterness of her doubting that there was a God. For what loving God would do that to a little baby? Or was this her punishment for surrendering to passion? This was the time when she and Melvin should have turned to each other. But Melvin never believed the doctors' conclusion. "Look at him," Melvin said as they stood, one on each side of the crib. "Prettiest baby I ever seen. Ain't nothing wrong with him."

Azuree shifted her gaze from Little Gene's vacuous face to Melvin's bland smile. "Shit," Melvin was saying, "them doctors don't know. Babies grow in their own time. Ain't nothing wrong with Daddy's boy. Look at him, just as healthy and pretty as can be." Melvin picked up Little Gene and started to hug him. But he quickly handed the baby to Azuree. "Here, he needs a change." And Melvin was off to wherever he went evenings, and she was left clutching a year-old child who had never sat up by himself and was greatly in need of a change.

Little Gene grew more beautiful every day, with smooth brown skin, big luminous eyes, a perfectly formed head covered with curly dark hair. Her love was all-engulfing and tinged with a deep-seated sense of guilt. Melvin was more and more distant, and finally, in the child's second year, he left.

Had she taken the time to notice Melvin, she would have anticipated his final solution to the problem. For Melvin was as transparent as gauze. He spent more and more time away from home. "Going over to Marian's," he would say. Marian was the oldest sister, the one who had taken him to live with her when their parents died. Marian was a buxom, aggressive woman, a deaconess in the church where, apparently, God pointed out the evil people whom He told His flock to chastise and avoid. She, Azuree, was evidently among the evil. After awhile, Melvin stopped saying where he was going—he just came home from work, nodded a curt greeting to Azuree, avoided looking at Little Gene, ate a silent supper, and went out. When he came home to bed, sex was not worth the effort. In her preoccupation with Little Gene, Azuree hardly noticed whether or not Melvin was there.

After he had left them, she did miss his ghostly presence. Meager as his income had been, it was at least something. Now there was nobody to help, not even her in-laws. With Little Gene in her arms, she approached them one by one, but each swore that nobody knew where Melvin was, and they reproached her, silently or directly, as being the reason that their Baby Bro had disappeared. And no, they didn't have any money to spare. Marian— the last one Azuree approached and then out of desperation—did not even invite her in. Arms folded over her pugnacious bosom and eyes spitting fire, Marian added to the family litany the fact that nobody believed that Little Gene was Melvin's child: he was too dark, and they didn't have any idiots in their family. Azuree stood there with her mouth agape for all of ten seconds. Then the floodgate of her resentment burst and even the invincible Marian stepped back, aghast at the quiet, subdued woman's venom. Even the slam of the door in her face could not slow the cascade of Azuree's curses.

Little Gene's loud cries interrupted her tirade, and amazed that he had finally responded to something other than his own body, she groped her way down the front steps and started the long walk home, still muttering curses.

Was it then, she wondered now, listening to Little Gene's soft breathing beside her, was it then that she knew what ultimately she must do?

Well, no use dragging all that stuff up now. She wiped her eyes on a corner of the shawl and held the child closer, trying to warm him. He wriggled in his sleep, and his head brushed her breast. Instinctively, she cringed. Although there was no pain yet, she protected that breast because of the lump, the poisonous mass of putrid flesh that foreshadowed her doom. She touched the bottle in her pocket and was comforted.

Now she drifted into an uneasy sleep with troubled dreams.

Images from the last five nightmarish years darted from some obscure part of her, combined into weird patterns, and faded, only to rise again in new and frightening combinations: a series of welfare workers, clean, white, and disdainful, leered at her; the crowded clinic where young receptionists called her by her first name became a jumble of noise and stench; the various bosses she had worked for when she could find somebody to take care of the child stared at her reprovingly, for she never kept a job long, because nobody would long take care of a four-year-old, or five-year-old, or six-year-old who couldn't feed himself and was still in diapers. And Little Gene himself penetrated her dreams, always the same at any age, the same beautiful face devoid of expression and intelligence, until finally in her dream the dead eyes became lit with hell-fire, and the sagging mouth curled into a satanic grin, and the child laughed at her, mocked her. And through it

all rang her death knell: "Cancer...too late...
cancer...." She awoke suddenly and came to herself
sitting upright, the child's fiendish laughter and the
dread pronouncement reverberating in her head in a
symphony of death.

Dusk of dawn. The day had come, the day she
had planned. It was the plan that had finally
promised peace. For the first time, in this one daring
act, she would be in control. Life would no longer
manipulate her. She would be the one to make the
choice. And now she touched the bottle in her pocket.
For her child she would defy God himself.

The cow mooed in lethargic indignation.
Clumsily, Azuree struggled to her feet and took a few
stiff steps. Then she knelt beside the child, who had
awakened and was gazing at her. "Morning,
Funny-Face," she whispered, smiling. " Yeah, it's me.
You ain't never gonna-wake up in that place, never
no more."

She recalled the awful day when she knew that
she had neither the strength nor the know-how to
care for the growing child, that she would never be
able to hold a job and provide for the two of them if
she kept the child. She had hoped that the
institution— Children's Home, they called it—would
be better than she thought, might even be able to
teach him to do some things for himself. But time
and time again she would find the child in a soggy
diaper, his brown skin looking a sickly yellow. To her
timid inquiries the director, a brusk middle-aged
white woman, would reply crisply, "We do the best
we can here, Mrs. Fisher. We're short-handed, and
he requires a lot of care; he can't do much anything"
For the first time the child was responding to his
surroundings: he began to whimper when she left
him.

There was nobody to whom she could turn for
advice or for a sympathetic ear. Joetta and Junie

had no reality for her, and being shy and withdrawn, she had made no friends on the job. Except for Little Gene, she was alone, left to deal with her hideous dilemma. More and more, she crept within herself. On the job she spoke only when necessary, ate her lunch alone and then stopped eating lunch at all. Many nights sleep would not come. She became gaunt and sunken-eyed. And as long as she could still carry bed pans, nobody noticed. She found a drop of comfort in an occasional bottle of wine. On paydays she would treat herself to a little Chianti or cheap Burgundy. Then, for a day or two, she had something to come home to: a bottle of tranquility awaited her. For a night or two she would sleep.

"Poor little lamb," Azuree muttered, remembering. She picked up the child and moved wearily to the open door. "Mama gon change you in a minute." She knew that farm people rose early, and her plan would be thwarted if she were discovered. She wondered whether the people at the home had even missed Little Gene. She had simply taken him and, when nobody was watching, walked out. She wondered grimly whether they even knew he was gone.

She cast a quick glance back into the barn. The cow, having voiced her objection to the intruders, was suckling her calf. Inexplicably, tears rose to Azuree's eyes. She left the barn and began the final steps of her journey.

The morning air was sweet, and in spite of the tortured night, Azuree felt refreshed. Her decisions were all made now, and nothing was ever going to hurt her child. *"Hush, little baby, don't you say a word,"* she sang to Little Gene, *"Papa's gonna buy you a mockingbird."*

Azuree knew these woods, at least as far as the stream. She had done domestic work for the wife of the farmer whose barn had sheltered them in the long night, and once or twice she had wandered into the woods at the end of the day. The woods were peaceful and welcoming. In the sheltering shadows she had found momentary respite from loneliness, fear, toil, and heartache. And, ultimately, the woods had provided the solution to all her problems.

The plan had been evolving for a long time, growing plainer as the years passed and Little Gene fell farther behind, but it came to her suddenly whole on a sleepless night after the doctor had sentenced her to death. *She* would decide the time, the place, and the manner of her death. She—not chance.

*"If that mockingbird don't sing,"* she continued joyously, *"Papa's gonna buy you a diamond ring."*

The outside world was becoming more and more remote. She looked back on it like one who is on the outside looking at some absurd, alien place. "That home wasn't no good nohow," she interrupted her song to mutter. "Sure wasn't no place you could call home." But it was all they had. She smiled bitterly at the trap in which she and Little Gene had been caught. First, the state had paid for the child's placement there. Now that she had gotten a better job her income was just enough to disqualify her for state aid—but not high enough for her to pay the prohibitive bill. She laughed shortly, then resumed her singing. *"If that diamond ring is brass, Papa's gonna buy you a looking glass."*

They had arrived at the place. A little stream flowed languidly, sunshine sparkling on its surface. Tiny transparent fish darted here and there, and a dragon fly hovered over the water lilies, its wings shining in the sun. "Now," Azuree muttered. "Now."

She spread the shawl on the soft grass beside the stream and laid Little Gene on it. She took off the backpack and rummaged inside it for the things she needed. A blue and black butterfly danced in the air,

and Azuree could have sworn that the child noticed,
that his eyes followed its airy flight. She smiled
tenderly. "It's all right now, baby. We gon be all
right." Tenderly she undressed Little Gene, her
hands gentle and loving. He shuddered briefly in the
morning chill. She folded the shawl lightly over the
emaciated body. She drew a washcloth from the
diaper bag, dipped the cloth into the stream, and
washed the child, uncovering one part of his body at
a time, then gently covering that part again in the
shawl. Softly she sang a song wrung from her
ancient unknown ancestors: "They crucified my
Lord, and he never said a mumbling word...not a
word...not a word...."

When she had washed him clean she dressed
him in the new clothes she had bought for this time
out of time. Then she wrapped him again in the
shawl. This time she wrapped him tightly, pinioning
his arms and legs. When he was all wrapped except
for his face, she hesitated. It was not too late. She
could take him back to the home. And then what?
She looked deeply into the dull eyes and in them she
read his future. Gently, with love, she drew the
shawl over his face and wrapped the shawl and
wrapped it, until there was no opening for air.
Kneeling back on her heels, she held the child
tenderly, rocking gently and whispering, "They laid
him in the tomb, and he never said a mumbling
word...." Held him through the muffled cries, held
him until the feeble struggle ended, held him and
sang to him until the shawl was damp with her
tears. Held him long after the little body was still,
and her song had ended. Held him silently in the
sunshine, in the soft, fragrant grass.

It was done. It was accomplished. She had given
life and she had snatched it away. She had broken
the commandment of God—"Thou shalt not kill, thou
shalt not kill." She had risked her eternal soul to
give her child the gift of death, her poor hurt child,

whom God would have set adrift in an uncaring world. For a moment, crouching beside the still water, she was stunned by the enormity of what she had done—and by its finality. Then, still holding the silent bundle, she reached into her pocket and drew out the little bottle which contained eternal peace. Sleeping pills carefully hoarded for months from prescriptions of different doctors. She popped two into her mouth—but her mouth was dry, and they wouldn't go down. She laid the child upon the grass and knelt beside the stream. She cupped her hands and drank of the healing waters. And the pills went down. All of them. When they were gone, she dropped the bottle into the stream and watched it disappear.

She took up the child again, and she waited. She closed her eyes and rocked back and forth, and she sang again to the child. "Sweet little Jesus boy...they didn't know who you was...." And there was no past, and there was no future only the strange and incomprehensible now.

Finally, she rose. She unwrapped the child and flung the shawl from her. She cradled him in her arms. My, he was really sleeping sound. Well, it was time to go, though she couldn't remember why or where. Still cradling him, she began to walk deeper into the woods. No tears now. For her spirit was at peace. She glanced at her child's beautiful face and felt a rush of gladness. She walked deeper and deeper into the woods, treading earth without pathways, where only wild things lived. And the birds welcomed them with song, and the sun warmed them, and insects buzzed cheerily. On and on she trudged, into the woods' shady heart. "Lord, Little Gene, you sure done got heavy," she murmured to the child in her arms, not in a complaining tone, but rather with an air of wonderment.

And for the first time that she could remember, her soul was deeply, profoundly at peace.

# *Dead Man Running*

S hackled, Jazzy avoided looking at the jury. His eyes followed the prosecutor, a young black woman with a neat Afro. He looked at nobody else. At fifteen, a dropout by choice, an illiterate by circumstance, a drug pusher by profession, Jazzy was an eyewitness to murder.

---

"It's them! Run, boys!" Red Man had cried out when they heard the shots. But by then the two hoods were upon them, the 9-millimeter semiautomatics precluding flight. Jazzy recognized them immediately: Nick and Stud, two dealers who had owned this territory until Red Man the New Yorker had moved in.

"Kick out the shit!" Nick demanded.

"Fuck you!" cried Red Man. In wild desperation he turned and dashed across the street toward a break in the row of houses, an empty space where a housed had once stood, a space like a gap in a snaggle-tooth mouth. If he could make the alley behind the row houses, he could leap the fence and be gone.

But the 9-millimeters spit death and an instant before safety a bullet ripped into Red Man's back, tore through his left lung and through his heart; then spent, dropped into the front of his heavy winter jacket. Somehow Red Man's body kept on running, a dead man running.

He staggered into the alley and smashed into the fence, where he collapsed, the shattered heart struggling for one more beat, the blood dyeing the jacket scarlet.

*"Kick out the shit!"* Nick yelled at the trembling Jazzy and his partner Joe. They fumbled nervously in their pockets, then thrust the little bags and the money at Nick. Some of the bags fell to the sidewalk, as Nick and Stud scrambled to retrieve them, Jazzy and Joe fled. Then the pop-pop-pop of gunshots...

Small and wiry, Jazzy slid under a car. He lay on his stomach shaking violently, the car's bottomside crushing him into the asphalt. His heart thudded and his breath heaved so loudly that he feared that anyone on the street might hear. With shaking fingers he flicked the cold sweat from his eyes.

Running footsteps! Nick or Stud! *Shit! They musta seen me!* The footsteps came louder. The ground shook with the pounding of feet on pavement. In his terror, Jazzy bit into his lower lip and tasted blood. His eyes stared into the darkness, expecting the muzzle of a gun to be thrust under the car, the flash of an explosion—

But the footsteps passed and receded. Jazzy waited until his heart quieted and his breath slowed. He peered out. The street was empty; the familiar midnight calm, ominous and pregnant with danger, had settled in. Cautiously he struggled out from under the car and for a moment crouched there, staring wildly in all directions. The only motion he saw was the blinking on and off of the Christmas lights around windows and doorways—red, blue, white, on and off in orderly sequence. Panic overwhelmed him, and he ran—back through the silent and murderous streets, back toward the nearby bar, where he could blend with the crowd.

What now? What now? In a few violent seconds, way less than a minute, his life had been forever changed. As long as Nick was on the streets, Jazzy was as good as dead.

---

"And did you recognize one of the gunmen? the prosecutor was asking.

"Yeah."

"Is he in the courtroom?"

"Yeah. He's here."

"Would you point out that person?"

"It's him." Jazzy pointed to Nick, sitting coolly beside his attorney, all decked out in a new brown suit.

The prosecutor said, "Let the record show that the witness has indicated the defendant."

Jazzy glanced briefly at the jury, then back to Nick, whose bland expression did not change. He might have been some youthful preacher listening to confessions.

---

*On the day before the trial began, a troubled child awoke at 3:30 A.M. He was not a good sleeper; he had too much on his mind. His parents had been bugging him again about cutting school. His parents were stupid. They couldn't see that he was a man now and would do as he chose. At thirteen he was not a kid anymore. He did the things that men do, and that made him a man. Already clothed—having felt the urgent need for one of his midnight prowls—he tiptoed down the steps (avoiding the creaky second step from the bottom) and slipped out the front door.*

*The child sauntered down the silent streets, hand in his pockets, fingers caressing the little plastic* bags. The lamplight cast dim shadows, which wavered in the sharp light of a passing car. He turned the corner and headed toward the Avenue, where the streets never sleep. The block was long, broken by an alley or two. In the lamplight the row of white marble steps were like gray ghosts crouched ominously in front of each house.

A couples of houses this side of the Avenue he saw her sitting on the steps waiting—for him or for whatever John came along. He slowed his pace and swaggered toward her. He was a man now. She had told him that he was a man. A few whispered words, then he followed her into the house. Afterward he paid her in crack.

As he left, the woman lingered a moment in the vestibule, clutching her precious little package and peering out from the shadows. At the bottom of the steps a man stopped the child. The long barrel of a gun glinted in the lamplight. The child gasped and took a step backward. Then, knowing that she was watching, he resumed his air of arrogance. He was not a kid now; he was Batman, he was Superman.

The man with the gun growled, "Gimme the stuff, mother fucker."

The child glanced toward the doorway where she stood and replied loudly enough for the woman to hear, "I wouldn't give you shit, motherfucker, if you stuck that gun in my mouth halfway down my throat!"

The man grabbed him by his jaw and pulled him close. The child smelled the stench of the sweaty arm pits. The man stuck the gun into the child's mouth. And before he could scream or even gag, the man fired.

---

Jazzy nervously clenched and unclenched his fists, and the chains jangled. Nick's lawyer, a balding white man in a rumpled gray suit, was pacing back and forth in front of the witness stand, shooting questions like bullets.

"And what where you doing at that intersection on the evening of December 27?"

"We was selling drugs, me and Joe."

"What did you do when Mr. Ortiz—uh, Red Man—arrived on the scene?"

"We give him the money."

"That was your usual practice?"

"Yeah."

"Was he alone?"

"No. Him and a guy name Herb come and collect money every little while."

"So you gave him the money?"

"Yeah."

"Minus you commission—your cut?"

"Yeah."

There was back-and-forth discussion about how much Jazzy had kept after giving the money to Red Man. Jazzy said several different amounts, but they were all considerably more than he would have earned working at McDonald's.

"What were you doing with all that money in your pocket?"

"That was *mine* man! That was *my money*!"

"Where was Herb all this time?"

"He never got out the car. I didn't see him after them guys come."

The lawyer made him recount the events of that night, questioning him on every detail, trying to trip him up in a lie.

"Where were you when you were taken for questioning in the early hours of December 28?"

"I was in a bar on the corner."

"What were you doing there?"

"I live there—in a room behind the bar."

"Who lives with you?"

"Nobody. I live by myself."

"Why did the detectives question you?"

"Because somebody told them they seen a young guy run into the bar, and I was the only young guy there."

"What did you tell the police about the events of that night?"

"I told them I didn't know nothing about no murder."

"And that was a lie, wasn't it?"

"Yeah, that was a lie."

---

By the time the police had released him, night had faded to a dirty gray dawn. Walking the shadowy streets, he was weary, confused, and frightened. His red eyes darted here and there searching for Nick. He had been numbed by the horror, but as the numbness wore off it was replaced first by disbelief, then by steadily mounting terror. The streets were his home, his pleasure, his livelihood—but now they were enemy territory. As his thoughts unraveled he wondered where Joe was and whether he, too, had been shot.

Jazzy ducked into a doorway, his heart booming like a drum: Nick! Nick coming toward him! Slowly, like he knew Jazzy couldn't get away! But the man who approached staggered slightly and kept on walking—some drunk trying to make it home. Jazzy exhaled loudly and moved on, still warily searching.

By now Jazzy was on home turf. He was known here. He had built a reputation here. A man huddled in doorway called to him. "Jazzy! Hey, Little Jazzy! Wait, man—" Jazzy kept walking. The man was trying to get up. Jazzy glanced at him. It was one of his many nameless customers. The man was skinny, a near-skeleton. "Jazz, wait—I need it bad. I got money. I can pay—" Jazzy kept walking, and the man screamed after him, "Shit-ass motherfucker!"

Red Man. Jazzy had seen death before, violent death. Who hadn't? Death didn't move him one way or the other. He had seen too much of it. But Red Man—Red Man had personified what Jazzy wanted to be. One of these days, Jazzy had promised himself, he too would wear expensive suits and gold chains and rings and watches, he too would ride around town in a Lexus, he too would have a fine bitch like Red Man's. Jazzy knew death, but he couldn't believe that Red Man was dead. Red Man was all that Jazzy had ever wanted to be.

It was broad daylight by now. A new day, though without sleep Jazzy wasn't sure where yesterday had ended and today had begun. Detectives were already in the street. He knew that he should get the hell out of there. But he was drawn to the place where his life had been changed forever.

A number of people were standing around looking, silent and wide-eyed. The cops were searching the pavement, street, and gutter for spent cartridges.

"Got one!" called a detective. The others came to look.

"Another shotgun shell. Looks like it's been there awhile, though."

"Yeah. Man, this place is a regular O.K. Corral!" The others laughed and went back to their search.

While the detectives were preoccupied, Jazzy retraced Red Man's steps through the break in the row of houses into the alley behind. The alley was cordoned off to keep onlookers away. A cop was there taking pictures of a chalk outline of Red Man's body.

A dark smear of blood covered the chest area. Jazzy recoiled as if the chalk outline were Red Man himself, then turned and trudged toward his room in back of the bar.

There was a Santa Claus or a star in every window, a Christmas wreath on every door. Someone had forgotten to turn off the lights around a doorway, and in the gray morning the lights blinked off and on, off and on—a lurid red, a red like the smear in the alley.

---

"When they questioned you again on December 31, did you then admit to having witnessed this crime?" Nick's lawyer was asking.

"Yeah. I told them about the robbery."

"And did you fail to identify my client's picture in the photographic line-up?"

"Yeah."

"I have here a copy of the police report in which you described the gunman as being short and light-skinned with brown hair. Now *look* at my client. Does that description fit him?"

Jazzy cast a quick glance at the tall, decidedly brown Nick sitting calmly as if he were a mildly interested spectator.

"No."

"You said that the gunman was a man called Doo-Doo. That was another lie, wasn't it?"

Jazzy paused. It wasn't a complete lie, he thought bitterly: Doo-Doo was another word for Shit. Then he answered, "Yeah."

"And you are lying now, aren't you, when you identify my client as the gunman."

"No. I'm telling the truth. It was him."

"Then why did you lie before when you failed to identify him and said that the gunman was somebody named Doo-Doo?"

Jazzy glanced at Nick's impassive face, all the more terrifying because of its lack of expression. Jazzy shuddered. "Because I was afraid for my life.

"What? We can't hear you."

"I was afraid for my life."

---

*On the afternoon of the first day of the trial a gaggle of kids were playing on Miz Mary's front steps. Meisha and Jo-Jo were playing jacks on the top steps. Kwame, Poochie and Butch were running around the steps playing cops and robbers. "Bang bang, you dead!" laughed Kwame, pointing a toy gun at Butch, who clutched his chest and dropped laughing onto the bottom step. Three little girls were jumping double-Dutch in front of the house. The toddler Big Guy was nearby watching them, laughing and jumping up and down on sturdy brown legs.*

> *Bluebells, cockle shells, every ivy over,*
> *If your teacher beats you, don't you cry...*

*At the first gunshot the children dropped their toys and dashed toward the house screaming. They knew the sound of gunshots. By the time they made the doorway, the street sounded like Fourth of July. Big Guy stumbled and fell as the older children, swept along by panic, scrambled by. Crying for his mother, Big Guy struggled alone up the steps as the sound of gunshots got louder. At the top step a final bullet went pop and Big Guy dropped, his head shattered. Before his frantic mother could reach him the white marble steps were stained with a puddle of slippery red.*

*Later that afternoon the police reported that Big Guy had been caught in crossfire between a drug*

*pusher and a customer who owed him money. The
fatal bullet was fired by the pusher—a lad of sixteen
whom police were trying to track down. The pusher
had at least a dozen addresses.*

*That night Big Guy's eighteen-year-old mother
gave birth to a daughter, born prematurely, who also
died.*

---

"And is it true," Nick's lawyer was saying, "that
on the third questioning, on January 4, you
identified Joseph Morton as your associate, who was
also present the night of the murder?"

"Yeah."

"And that it was not until *after* Joseph Morton
identified my client that you picked him out of a
photographic line-up?"

"Yeah."

"And that my client's picture was the only one
presented to you on both December 31 and January
4?"

"I don't know."

"If you lied to the police on two other interviews,
why do you think we should believe you now?"

"Because it's true. It's true. It was him."

"What is my client's name?"

"I don't know."

"But you say you know him."

"I don't know his name, but I seen him around
plenty. Joe used to sell drugs for him."

"Objection! Move to strike!" shouted the lawyer.

"Sustained," said the judge, a sharp-eyed woman
who had seen much of the city's underside. "The jury
will disregard the remark about Joe."

Nick's lawyer turned back to Jazzy, his voice
deceptively quiet. "After you picked my client's

picture out of the lineup, police could not locate you at the address you had given. Where were you?"

"I moved."

"Where?"

"Lots of places. I didn't want nothing more to do with this thing."

"Why are you in custody now?"

"The police took me in for attempted auto theft."

"When?"

"About a week ago."

The lawyer moved closer. He put his elbow on the witness stand near Jazzy's face. His voice dropped to a tone of intimacy. "What were you promised in exchange for your testimony?"

"She said after I testified I could go home."

"What *she*?"

"Her." Jazzy pointed to the prosecutor.

"She told you that if you said that Nick killed Red Man you would be released?"

"Objection!" cried the outraged prosecutor, leaping to her feet.

"Sustained. Approach the bench."

On redirect, the prosecutor established that Jazzy was being held as a material witness and that after the trial he would be released whatever his testimony.

The first day ended. Jazzy shuffled from the courtroom, his chained fists flopping awkwardly against his thighs. His steps were small, mincing lady-steps because his feet were linked by chains. At every step the chains jangled.

---

*On the evening of the first day, a local television station did an investigative report on the properties of David Meyers, the city's most affluent slumlord.*

*The Health Department had long since condemned
some of his holdings as unfit for human habitation.
But for whatever reasons, no city agency had checked
to see whether repairs had been made or tenants
evicted. In fact, the condemned properties were
inhabited: They were inhabited by Black people.*

*The merciless camera revealed the squalor of the
lives condemned to those prison-houses. When the
floodlights lit up a dark kitchen, roaches fled in all
directions. A rat, blinded by the light, interrupted his
feast of garbage and ran helter-skelter seeking his
hole, chirping angrily. The camera panned through a
dark hallway to a bedroom, revealing bare walls,
floors, and doorframes gray with ground-in dirt.
Inside the bedroom a gray sheet covered a lumpy
mattress, and clothes and debris littered the floor. An
ancient woman, from whose head finger-long plaits
stuck out like spikes, sat rocking and gazing out of
the screenless window oblivious to the camera; the
soft creak-creak of the chair seemed to establish an
orderly rhythm in the chaos of that room. The camera
moved into the bathroom. Rust marks mottled the
sink and tub. The wooden toilet was splintered and
stained.*

*The reporter was a young blond woman, crisply
efficient but obviously repelled by what she had seen.
Standing at the foot of the unpainted wooden steps,
she talked with a tenant, a thin middle-aged woman,
who stood with her arms folded in front of her chest.*

*"We don't use the bathroom much anyways," the
woman was saying in answer to a question. "The
water don't work in there. We wash ourselves in the
kitchen. We all use the toilet and when it smell too
bad someone—me mostly—carry water from the
kitchen to flush it. Yes'm, I told Mr. Dave, but he ain't
got around to fixing it yet."*

*An adolescent girl sat on the bottom step, legs
akimbo, sucking her thumb. Beside her crouched a*

spindly-legged baby about a year old, grasping an empty nursing bottle and now and then chewing on the nipple.

"It's better than the last place," the woman continued. "Rats was so bad in the bathroom that we was 'fraid to use the toilet. We used a bucket in the kitchen and after 'while we'd empty it in the toilet and run." She smiled nervously.

"Mrs. Brown, couldn't you do something to get rid of the roaches and the rats?"

"What you gon do? They all up in the walls, up in the ceilings and down there under the floors. Yes, we put down baking soda and all for the roaches and set out traps for the rats and plug up the holes when we can find 'em." She pushed a lock of graying hair from her forehead, then folded her arms again. "But the more you kill, the more comes on. Mr. Dave don't own this place—" she chuckled bitterly— "they does—the roaches and the rats."

The camera picked up a boy of about twelve standing in the doorway scowling. The woman glanced at him and said, "That one learned to count by figuring how many roaches he done squashed." The boy shot her a baleful glance, then withdrew into the house.

"How much rent do you pay for this place?" the reporter asked.

"Three hundred and sixty-five dollars every month."

"Why don't you just move?"

"Where at? They all about the same."

The reporter ended with a close-up of the baby's face, solemn and already old.

---

The second day of the trial began with a surprising development. When the jury filed in after a forty-minute delay, Jazzy, chained, was on the stand about to be questioned by Nick's lawyer. The judge explained to the jury that on the previous day, a most unusual thing had happened: Despite her orders to the contrary, Jazzy and Nick, along with Herbert Benson, Joseph Morton and their guards, were together on the same elevator as they were returning to the lock-up. The ancient elevator had gotten stuck between floors, and for an hour and a half the adversaries were confined together in a space almost as cramped as a grave. The jury was not told what had transpired there, except for a small bit of testimony from Jazzy.

The defense attorney could hardly contain his triumph. "Now," he said, bouncing out of his chair beside Nick and striding briskly to the witness stand. He elicited from Jazzy the facts which the judge had already stated, then—

"And did you have conversation with my client?"

"Yeah."

"Who began the conversation?"

Jazzy darted a quick glance at Nick, sitting comfortably and poker-faced behind the defense's table. "He did."

"What did my client say to you?"

"He said, 'Why did you *finger* me?'"

"He asked you why you had identified *him*?" The jury, fascinated by this unusual development, missed the defense attorney's subtle shift in emphasis.

"Yeah."

"I have no more questions, Your Honor." The defense attorney turned his back to Jazzy and returned to his place beside Nick.

"No questions," muttered the prosecutor, and Jazzy was led from the courtroom, his chains jingling like sleigh bells.

Not until the trial was over did any of the jurors recall that Herb, who had been with Red Man on the night of the murder, had been held as a witness but had never been called.

The next witness was Joe, who at nineteen was in the penitentiary for drug distribution. Tough and surly, Joe gave essentially the same account of the murder. His manner was more defiant than Jazzy's, more openly hostile. None of the jurors recalled Jazzy's statement that Joe had once sold drugs for Nick before the advent of Red Man; Joe, too, was manacled.

The defense had few questions for Joe, who had readily identified Nick's photograph in the line-up. Nick, during the testimony, regarded Joe with cool contempt. In contrast to Joe's tee shirt, jeans, and chains, Nick wore his new brown suit with a pale yellow shirt and brown figured tie. As Joe shuffled off the stand, Nick sat tall. He was dignified and handsome. He could have been the son of almost any member of the jury.

The rest of the prosecution's case was testimony from the medical examiner and the law enforcement officials. Their testimony compressed a man's life into a residue of statistics and bald facts. The medical examiner, a middle-aged woman with a thick German accent, gave Red Man's age, 27, and his weight and height, and described his general state of health. She said dryly that his left arm had old scars consistent with needle pricks and that a bullet, now covered with scar tissue, had lodged in his left lung, apparently from a wound inflicted years back. The jurors were passed a photograph of Red Man after autopsy, a handsome young man cut up and sewn together like a crazy-quilt. A neat little hole was in his chest. His eyes were closed as if in sleep.

*At about the time the second day of the trial ended, a missing sixteen-year-old was found. Her name was Tiffany. Her photograph had been shown on television and in the newspapers, a pretty little thing smiling broadly into the camera. Her hair was piled high in a kind of cone, with all sorts of whirls and swirls and streaks of fuschia. Fancy earrings dangled to her shoulders. She seemed to be enjoying a good joke. Her mother and grandmother, stunned by this unbelievable thing, tearfully insisted that she had been abducted, but the police were convinced at first that she was another teen runaway. Three days after her disappearance her mother revealed that Tiffany was four months pregnant, whereupon her boyfriend, an unemployed twenty-year old neighbor, had been questioned and released.*

*As Nick's jury was filing out of the courtroom, an elderly man was walking his German Shepherd at the edge of a wooded area in Druid Hill Park. Something in the woods attracted the dog, and she jerked the lead from the old man's hand and dashed into the trees. Calling the dog and cursing, the man stumbled along behind her, deeper and deeper into the woods. Under a thick oak, nestled in a bed of last winter's leaves, the man made a hideous discovery: A girl in her teens, fully clad in jeans and a tee shirt stiff with blood, her wide eyes staring at death. She wore no earrings now—there were gashes on her lobes where the earrings had been torn from her—and her hair was a wild tangle around her face. Her hands were tied behind her, execution-style.*

On the third day of the trial the defense presented two witnesses, Nick's women. The first was the mother of Nick's three-year-old son. She had brought the child to court. As she walked up the aisle she dropped the child off with a middle-aged woman and an elderly man, who gripped a crutch. These were obviously Nick's mother and grandfather, who had sat tensely through each day of the trial. The child came to them readily.

The child's mother, an attractive brown-skinned woman in her early twenties, testified that Nick had spent Christmas with her and the child, and that on the morning before the murder he had left her house because he had become ill and they did not want the child to catch his sickness. He told her that he was going to the hospital emergency room for treatment.

The second defense witness, Nick's current girlfriend, took up the story from there. She was a frightened-looking woman of no more than twenty. She testified that the father of her six-year-old son had spent Christmas with her but on the day in question had taken the child to spend a few days with his family. Nick had called her from the hospital and said that he had not been examined but that he was too sick to wait any longer. She told him he could come to her house. He stayed there for several days, during which time she had no visitors and no one saw him there. At the time of the murder he was at her house feverish and vomiting.

Neither witness looked at the jury. As they testified, Nick permitted himself a slight smile and an occasional nod.

The defense rested.

The prosecutor's summation was brief. She could make no mention of the theory which she had presented initially—that Nick was a rival drug dealer—since no testimony to that effect had been generated. The jury could not be told that Joe had refused to testify on that point, and Herb had refused to testify at all, their rights being protected by the Fifth Amendment. So the case for the prosecution depended upon whether the jury believed the eyewitness accounts of Jazzy and Joe.

The defense attorney's summation contained a
surprise that jerked the jury awake.

"Ladies of the jury," he began—for the jury was
composed of women, ten black and two white, all
professional women—"let me remind you that the
defense needed to present no case at all. The
presumption of innocence is the cornerstone of our
American judicial system: A person is innocent until
proven guilty. *Until proven guilty!* We do not need to
prove innocence—it is up to the prosecution to prove
guilt. Ladies of the jury, the prosecution has not
done that. She has presented *not one piece of
evidence* to link my client with this crime except the
word of two street thugs and drug pushers,
testimony which is simply not to be believed. If the
victim had been shot *before* he got to the alley and to
the fence where he was found, there should have
been a trail of blood. *Where was that trail?* It was not
there!

"Now I will tell you what really happened that
night. Red Man was murdered right there in the
alley—*by Jazzy and Joe!* That is why there was no
trail of blood. That is why no money was found on
Red Man's body. Because he was shot to death right
there in that alley by the same two hoodlums who, to
save themselves, concocted that *fairy tale* to put the
blame on my client. Ladies, I ask you to open the
way for prosecution of the *real* murderers.

I ask you to find my client *not guilty!*"

The judge's instructions were clear. She defined
each of the charges. If the jury found that the
murder was committed in the course of a robbery
and that the defendant was one of the robbers, then
he was guilty whether or not he pulled the trigger.
The jury was to consider only that which was
actually presented as evidence *and nothing else*. The
fact that the defendant chose not to testify was not
to be considered an admission of guilt. Also, the jury

must not consider the consequences of releasing the defendant back into the community. Nor was the defendant's past history relevant to the present charges. *Only the evidence in this crime was to be considered.* If that evidence left the jury with a reasonable doubt, then the defendant must be found not guilty.

The jury's deliberations were fairly brief. From the beginning, most could not put any credence in the testimony of Jazzy and Joe, certainly not enough to convict anybody of murder. For some, the defense attorney had planted a reasonable doubt: In the stalled elevator Nick *had* asked Jazzy why he had identified *him* and not someone else, and if Jazzy and Joe had committed the murder, then they would certainly blame *somebody*. In the absence of hard evidence the verdict rested simply on whom one should believe. And no humane person would condemn someone, especially a young person, to years— perhaps a lifetime—in prison on evidence so flimsy as the word of two known street thugs and drug pushers. And nobody wants to look upon a clean, open-faced young person and believe that his is the face of a murderer.

Few if indeed any of the jurors would have admitted to the small voice that whispered just below consciousness; *It's late and I'm tired and I want to get home. . . After all, Red Man was a drug dealer; let them kill each other. . .*

The jury found Nick not guilty of all charges.

Everyone's eyes were on Nick's triumphant grin, on the relieved smiles of his mother and grandfather (though they made no move to embrace him), and on the defense attorney's cool acceptance of yet another victory. Nobody noticed that the young woman with the baby, who had attended the trial each day, left the courtroom silently, her head down, her eyes filling with angry tears. And nobody noticed the

187

prosecutor's stricken face. It was she who had
persuaded Jazzy to testify, she who had promised
that his testimony would send Nick to prison. Joe, in
the penitentiary, was safe from Nick's
vengeance—but the streets would offer Jazzy no
sanctuary.

---

The trial over, Jazzy was released into a
dangerous freedom. Death was out there somewhere,
waiting.

The wellspring of rage within Jazzy had swollen
to a cataract of swirling emotions. He walked rapidly
up Fayette Street, away from the courthouse, away
from the pristine world of oak and marble, back to
the world which had spawned him, where each
denizen was both prey and predator, where even
children were both fearful and feared. Courage
misdirected. Love distorted. Rage turned inward.
For they were heirs to centuries-long hatred and
oppression but not to their forebears' faith and
fortitude. Faith and fortitude are, in the long run,
flimsy defense—and no offense at all.

Two women approaching Jazzy from the opposite
direction clutched their purses and drew closer
together.

Jazzy breathed deeply the essence of a June
night in the city. The rush hour was over now, the
downtown crowds vanished, the streets ominously
still. He tried to unravel his thoughts into a coherent
plan to escape Nick's revenge. But he could not
think. He felt as if there were a coil inside his chest,
wound too tight. He broke into a trot; then without
any conscious decision, he began running, running
back to the old neighborhood, back to the death that
waited behind some white marble stairway, between
parked cars, or in the bowels of some
alley...running...running...running....